About the author

Maria Tippett has written more than a dozen books, many of them on themes in Canadian and British cultural history. Her classic biography, *Emily Carr, a biography,* still in print today, received the Governor General's Award in Canada. Other landmark publications include her ground-breaking study, *By a Lady: celebrating three centuries of Canadian Women in the visual arts*; and her *History of Sculpture in Canada* further extended her range. She has curated numerous exhibitions in North America and in Europe and contributed to arts documentaries. Her aptitude for writing fiction was shown in an earlier book of short stories, *Breaking the Cycle and other stories from a Gulf Island.* She held the Robarts Chair of Canadian Studies in Toronto and was a senior research fellow at Churchill College, Cambridge University. She and her husband, the British historian, Peter Clarke, now divide their time between Pender Island in British Columbia and Cambridge in the United Kingdom.

ART FOR ART'S SAKE

MARIA TIPPETT

ART FOR ART'S SAKE

Vanguard Press

A CIP catalogue record for this title is
available from the British Library.

ISBN 978 1 80016 413 0

Vanguard Press is an imprint of
Pegasus Elliot Mackenzie Publishers Ltd.
www.pegasuspublishers.com

First Published in 2022

Vanguard Press
Sheraton House Castle Park
Cambridge England

Printed & Bound in Great Britain

Dedication

For Fay Bendall

Contents

Inconspicuous Consumption

I could begin this tale in 1900. That's the year when Paris hosted the *Exposition Universelle*, with such great international publicity and acclaim. The fair was the place to be seen and, in keeping with Thorstein Veblen's concept of "conspicuous consumption", the place to be seen spending money. It was also where the owner of the largest slaughterhouse in Chicago had bought his first picture.

Since I've got a walk-on part in this story, I'm going to begin this tale in 1940. That was the last full year of peacetime for the United States. The year that Franklin Roosevelt got re-elected president with a promise to keep America out of "foreign wars". And, most important of all for me, the year that I, Robert Cunliffe, met Charlotte Henley.

I was looking for a summer job before taking up post-graduate studies at Harvard University. As it turned out I didn't have to look far. Three houses down the road, the widow of the meat-packer extraordinaire, Arthur J. Henley – who had succumbed to a nasty bout of pneumonia a couple of years earlier – needed help cataloguing her paintings and drawings.

No one in Chicago knew what kind of art Arthur and Charlotte Henley had been collecting since their second visit to Paris in 1901. But no one doubted that there must be plenty of it since they'd built an enormous steel and glass-roofed art gallery beside their lakeside mansion. The contents of this miniature version of Paris's *Grand Palais* were a mystery to my parents and me, to other residents living in Oak Park and even to the director of the Art Institute of Chicago who liked to boast that he'd seen every work of art that hung on every wall in the city.

Arthur Henley and his wife, Charlotte, liked to keep it that way. They didn't give a damn about advancing their own social status by opening their collection to their neighbours, art officials or to the general public. They had a firm grasp of who they were. And because it was their *inconspicuous* enjoyment of their artistic acquisitions that mattered to them, it was not surprising that Mrs Henley offered me the job on one condition. 'It's yours, Robert, if you can keep the contents of the gallery a secret.' Desperate to see what that monstrosity of a building contained, I immediately agreed.

***

Rumour had it that Arthur Henley was crude and uneducated. For how could a man who had transformed his father's two-barn abattoir into a multi-million-dollar business by paying his employees less than half a living wage and by wrapping the city in a thick layer of greasy ink-black smoke, be otherwise? This was the unflattering view of the Henleys that I shared along with everyone else in town — until I walked into the foyer of the Henley gallery.

The first thing I saw was a head-and-shoulders bust of a man who appeared to be in his early thirties. He had finely chiselled features and a broad, across-the-face smile. And he wore a floppy fedora that made him look more like Franz Hals' *Laughing Cavalier* than the hard-nosed businessman who had turned ten thousand cattle a day into steaks and ground beef.

'Rodin did that in one sitting,' Mrs Henley told me as she swept a bangle-clad arm towards the sculpture of her late husband. I was duly impressed, as she doubtless expected of an aspiring student of the history of art.

If I had hoped to see more busts created by Rodin when I followed Mrs Henley into the body of the gallery, I would have been disappointed. True, there were settees covered in plush red velvet and a highly-polished Ormolu table. There were potted palms that dwarfed my six-foot tall height. And there were dozens of square and rectangular wooden crates stacked against the walls. All of this seemed highly decorous and conventional and I could well imagine it furnishing Rodin's turn-of-the-century salon.

Then, I looked above the crates. Mounted on the rose-coloured walls were hundreds of drawings, oil paintings and etchings. Some featured melancholic women and children. Others depicted Harlequins and copulating human-headed bulls. And there were several distinctive split-faced images of young women.

'You're no doubt familiar with the work of *this* artist,' Charlotte Henley commented briskly. True enough, she didn't have to tell me who had created these incredible paintings and drawings. The twentieth century's most famous painter had indeed been the subject of my graduating essay at the University of Chicago, as my neighbour probably knew. In fact, until I walked into the Henley's private gallery that early spring morning in 1940, I had convinced myself that I knew more about this artist than anyone else in Chicago.

'I spotted you in New York last spring at the Modern Museum of Fine Art,' Mrs Henley now revealed, with sly self-satisfaction.

It hadn't been difficult persuading Mother to take me to Pablo Picasso's first retrospective exhibition in North America. She had been as thrilled as I was about the prospect of seeing the Spanish artist's work in the flesh. After all, she was the one who possessed a Master's degree in twentieth century European painting — the person who had cultivated my own interest in art. Yet, as Mother and I moved from one picture to another around the Museum of Modern Art's vast galleries, it was me who had done most of the talking. Mother dutifully listened to my running commentary. She patiently watched me wave my arms before each work as though I was conducting a hundred-piece symphony orchestra. And, when a group of people took me for the gallery's docent and followed me around the exhibition like lost sheep, Mother had proudly stood on the fringes of the small crowd.

I had immediately wondered during my interview with Charlotte Henley whether she had likewise watched and listened to Chicago's self-proclaimed youthful expert hold forth on Picasso. The playful smile that spread across her face left no doubt in my mind that she had seen me holding forth at the Museum of Modern Art the previous spring. And that she didn't need any of my undergraduate insights into Picasso's work. In fact, all that Mrs Henley needed was my muscle, my agility and my record-keeping skills.

***

Over the course of those long summer months, I uncrated pictures that had been shipped to Chicago from Zurich, New York and also from war-torn Paris and London before Hitler had completed his invasion of continental Europe. I climbed a three-storey-high ladder and nailed a fourth row of pictures to the gallery's rose-coloured walls. And I applied my innate meticulousness to help Mrs Henley record the title, the dimensions, the medium and the condition of every work in the collection.

My parents had naturally been curious about the secrecy surrounding my employment. 'Fess up, Robert,'

Mother would ask, 'what's in that pretentious building anyway?' Equally curious, my father assured me that I would not betray Mrs Henley's trust if I revealed the contents of the gallery to my parents alone.

Initially I enjoyed keeping the Henleys' secret to myself, but soon found that I also enjoyed giving my parents a few hints. In any case, it was difficult for me to hide my excitement over the opportunity that I had been given. There was a visceral thrill in viewing a work that had never been exhibited, never been illustrated or put on the auction block; and I could not conceal this when I returned home at the end of the day. Mother would have revelled in discovering an unknown work by Picasso. After all, it was she who had taught me the importance of purchasing work directly from the artist, rather than buying one that was "second-hand" — or in art gallery parlance, *burnt*.

No, I did not reveal the name of the artist, but I did tell my parents how I recorded the details of every work in a large leather-bound ledger. I boasted about my agility in balancing on the precarious wooden ladder. I described the tuna salads that appeared on the mahogany ormolu table at precisely one o'clock every day. And I cherry-picked a few choice anecdotes to retell when I returned home.

I relished being the unique recipient of Mrs Henley's confidences. But I never told my parents how she and her husband had discovered Picasso. How they had walked into Picasso's first exhibition at the Galerie

Laffitte in 1901 and discovered the copies of old master paintings that he had made when he was a student at the Llotja School of Fine Arts in Barcelona. Nor did I reveal how Ambroise Vollard had sold the Henleys virtually every work from that exhibition and continued to sell them every work by Picasso for several years after that.

I naturally wondered why Mrs Henley and her husband had decided to invest in work by an unknown artist. 'Well, the prices were modest,' Mrs Henley acknowledged. But there was more to it than that. The Henleys found that Picasso's realistic drawings were entirely different from the muddy and garish Impressionist paintings that other wealthy Americans were collecting at the time. 'In fact,' Charlotte Henley continued, 'Arthur and I both felt that even if this young Spanish migrant from Malaga never produced another thing, we had paintings and drawings that were simply a privilege to view ourselves — still more a privilege to own.'

The joys of possession were never lost on the Henleys; and, of course, Picasso did produce more, much, much, much more. And Henry and Charlotte Henley took advantage of the artist's prodigious output on their annual visits to Paris. Until 1913, at any rate. That was the year that Picasso's abstract painting, *Woman with Mustard Pot,* was exhibited in Chicago at a watered-down version of New York's famous Armory show. The Henleys had attended that exhibition. And when Arthur Henley saw Picasso's abstract work on display, he had been shocked. He felt aesthetically betrayed by Picasso's "Cubist monstrosity", as the newspapers called *Woman with Mustard Pot*. And he felt financially duped because by this time he and Charlotte had bought more than three hundred paintings and drawings from Picasso's dealer, Ambroise Vollard.

'Fortunately, no one in Chicago knew what we were collecting,' Charlotte explained to me after two glasses of wine, 'otherwise Arthur would have felt even more foolish than he already did. After all, by 1913 we'd spent the previous twelve years accumulating Picasso's work. And we'd also built this gallery to house it. In the end,' Charlotte continued with a rueful smile, 'Arthur needn't have worried about being exposed as a fool because, at the outbreak of the First World War, Picasso put aside his Cubist style and returned to creating realistic pictures.'

Hearing this, I naturally reminded Mrs Henley that Picasso's foray into Neo-classicalism during the Great War was short-lived. But in the end, that hadn't made much difference to Arthur Henley. Indeed, when Picasso reverted to abstract painting following the First World, Arthur Henley was uncharacteristically philosophical. 'You see,' he had told his wife. 'We'll continue to collect Picasso's realistic work just to prove that he can really draw.' And that's what the couple had been doing up until Arthur Henley's death two years earlier.

I not only avoided telling my parents that the Henleys had a magnificent collection of work by Pablo Picasso, I never told them that the tuna salads I ate with Mrs Henley were accompanied by large glasses of vintage burgundy. Or how, after drinking a third glass of wine in the late afternoon, I would crank up the Edison phonograph that stood in the corner of the gallery, select one of Johann Strauss' waltzes, then, taking Mrs Henley in my arms, guide her around the crates, the velvet settees and the potted palms until the phonograph's needle had reached the centre of the record.

The dancing had been Mrs Henley's idea. I could have told her that I had two left feet. A tin ear. Or no sense of rhythm. But I'm glad that I didn't. And when we began to dance, I might have been repulsed by seeing Mrs Henley's liver-spotted hand on my shoulder, by feeling her sagging breasts when they brushed against my arms and by catching a close-up glimpse of her wrinkled neck. But instead, I quickly entered into the spirit of the occasion — and came to enjoy every minute.

Mrs Henley not only taught me how to waltz, she prompted me to look beyond the frame of a painting. I already knew that Picasso had been inspired by the work of early nineteenth-century French and Spanish painters and after that, by African mask-makers, along with his own contemporaries, Matisse and Modigliani. But, until meeting Charlotte Henley, I never paused to consider how Picasso had built his reputation. She told me how he had avoided participating in group exhibitions lest his own work was diminished by comparison with his fellow artists. How he had stuck to one dealer during his formative years. How he had kept his prices higher than his rivals. And how, when he began amassing a small fortune from the sale of his paintings, he had defied the image of the starving bohemian artist by riding in a chauffeur-driven Hispano-Suiza automobile, by wearing tailor-made suits, by living in an elegant apartment in Paris's 8th arrondissement and by acquiring a villa in the country.

'I sometimes wondered if Arthur was more impressed by Picasso's lifestyle and his shrewdness as a businessman, than he was by his art,' Mrs Henley revealed.

These revelations during our lunchtime, along with the dancing, persuaded me that Charlotte Henley and I were close. Yet we were not really close because by the end of the summer I was no nearer to discovering what everyone in Chicago was asking: what was the ultimate fate, whatever it contained, of the Henley Art Gallery?

As it turned out, I would never have a further opportunity to satisfy my curiosity, or to waltz around the gallery or to benefit from informal lessons in the social history of art. Because by the time I returned to Chicago, after my first year at Harvard, Charlotte Henley was dead. Her early and unexpected demise at the age of sixty-four two weeks previously had been as sudden as that of her husband. It came to me as a heavy blow. And it ended a brief though significant period of my life.

'Now that she's passed on, Robert,' my mother said shortly after I returned home, 'you're free to tell me what's in the collection.'

Dead or alive, Mrs Henley had exacted from me a promise that I did not feel that I should break, so I simply replied: 'Why don't you ask her son?'

***

I had not met Walter Henley the previous summer. But I had certainly seen him. Just after I had arrived for work, he'd be climbing into a chauffeur-driven limousine. It didn't take me long to figure out where he was going or why he was wearing overalls and a baseball cap. He could only be heading in one direction — to the great Henley family slaughterhouse on the other side of town.

A few days after I had returned from Boston, Walter asked me to meet him at the gallery. It was late afternoon. Enormous linen screens had been installed under the gallery's glass-domed ceiling. The horizontal sails diffused the light and made the paintings and drawings recede into their frames. There were other things that were also different. The potted palms and velvet settees had been removed. The sculpture of Arthur Henley and the ormolu table where I'd shared so many lunches with Walter's mother had been put into storage. And, of course, Mrs Henley was herself absent. As if to evoke his mother's presence, Walter uncorked a bottle of champagne, filled two glass flutes then said: 'Here's to Charlotte Henley.'

Though no more than a year older than me, Walter exuded the confidence of a wealthy businessman. He possessed his father's finely chiselled features, captured by Rodin so many years earlier, but they seemed out of sync with his corpulent figure. For Walter Henley was a large if not an obese man.

'I didn't know that my parents were collecting goddamn Picassos until I walked in here four years ago,' Walter said in a tough-guy argot that was better suited to the slaughterhouse than to the art gallery. 'And I probably wouldn't have known they were collecting Picassos, if father hadn't insisted on spending the final year of his life in this bloody place.'

Seeking to offer an explanation for his parents' secrecy, I told Walter how Japanese collectors believed that the value and beauty of their wood-cut prints diminished every time another person viewed them.

'Even if their one and only child viewed them?' Walter asked without expecting me to reply.

The conversation threatened to die on us. But I seized my opportunity by asking him what everyone in Chicago apparently wanted to know: 'So what's going to happen to the art collection now that your mother's gone? Are you planning on giving it to the Art Institute or to the University of Chicago? Or have you decided to open up this place to the public?'

'Nothing's going to happen!' Walter replied. 'Mother made it very clear in her will that I should continue to collect Picasso's work — especially the abstract canvases that she'd begun buying with a fury immediately after father's death.'

'So that's why you've contacted me?'

'No, I don't need your help to collect more Picassos, Robert. The dealers and auction houses have all of that in hand. And I can assure you that Mother certainly left enough money to keep those folks busy.'

Walter had resolved my immediate doubts about the future of the collection. But I still didn't know where I fitted in until he poured a second glass of champagne, then revealed: 'What I'd like you to do is to keep on doing what you did last summer.' I paused long enough to let him know that my labour could not be easily bought. Nor could my secrecy about the contents of the gallery simply be assumed. I still had my own qualms about whether I would now be free to tell my own parents exactly what I'd been uncrating and cataloguing and hanging the previous summer.

Even so, I did need a summer job. So, after a long pause I eventually replied: 'I'll continue if you get me a decent ladder.'

On these terms, I started to work again, just as before. Yet everything now seemed different. For one thing, I didn't realize how much I would miss Charlotte

Henley's soft voice or the girlish delight she had taken in watching me hang one of Picasso's abstract "monstrosities", which she had been buying since her husband's death, next to one of his representational paintings. I missed the tuna salads and those restorative glasses of red wine. And there was also the dancing.

But some of the loss that I experienced was compensated at the beginning of each day when I pulled back the gallery's lofty screens covering the glass dome. I greeted the paintings like old friends. When I wrenched open a newly arrived crate, I made new friends, too. And even though it was the famous fifteenth-century Italian Medici family that had consumed my scholarly interest at Harvard, I found that, back in Chicago, I never ceased to be overwhelmed by Picasso's prodigious energy and inventiveness and by his subtle line. But, without Mrs Henley, my job just wasn't the same.

Whether Walter sensed my loneliness, or just wanted to exercise his new-found right to enter the gallery at will, he made a habit of joining me when I took a short break at noon. While I ate sandwiches, prepared by mother the previous evening, and drank lukewarm coffee from a thermos, Walter nursed his own glass of wine rather than following his late mother's hospitable habits.

We soon discovered that we had more in common than our age, or the art collection or even Charlotte Henley. Walter and I had grown up in the same town —

and in the right part of it to boot. Admittedly, while I had the luxury of studying full-time, Walter had to share his academic ambitions with overseeing the family's investments in the meat-packing trade. And I thought it much to his credit that he had enrolled on a part-time course in the graduate school of business at the University of Chicago.

Walter and I also shared an antipathy to eastern Americans: 'You must have discovered by now that they're all snobs in Boston,' to which I nodded my head in agreement. 'And unlike us folks in Chicago,' Walter continued, 'too many of them want to get America involved in that war in Europe.' It was significant that, with the United States now increasingly making its own preparations to enter the Second World War, neither of us had enlisted in the armed forces. As the head of the slaughterhouse, Walter was deemed to be doing a vital job, whereas I was exempted from war service because at the age of fourteen a serious bout of pneumonia had scarred my lungs.

Walter did most of the talking during our lunches. He set out his plans for developing the family business after its long neglect by his art-struck parents. 'I'm spending the summer putting some of my recent studies into practice by asking the workers, *not* the managers, what they like and dislike about their jobs. I've built a large canteen in order to give every one of my employees a free lunch. And do you know what's happened, Robert? The company's productivity has increased by three per cent.'

While Walter talked about the newly recognized social responsibility of the businessman, I talked about how, during the fifteenth century, Italy's first art patrons had put sacred art into a profane setting. 'Are you suggesting that I follow the Medici family and hang a few Picassos around the slaughterhouse, Robert?'

Though our lunches were jovial, the fact that they took place in the gallery provoked some unpleasant memories for its new owner. 'During my childhood, my parents spent every darn evening in this place,' he explained. 'It wouldn't have been so bad if they'd limited their time here to the pre-dinner cocktail hour. But they chose to have their dinner here too. By the time I'd finished my supper in the kitchen and gone to bed, they'd still be here. God only knows what they got up to!'

I knew what Henry and Charlotte had been up to. They had danced. They had enjoyed knowing that they were the only people viewing their carefully selected pictures. And, I could also have told Walter, that his father had taken a great deal of pleasure from believing that he had saved Picasso's reputation by confining his purchases to "the Master's" realistic work. But I remained silent. Indeed, I felt some embarrassment in knowing that, during the previous summer, Walter's mother had evidently communicated far more freely with me than with her own son.

'And did you ever wonder what I was doing while you and Mother were eating your tuna salads and sipping your wine?' he asked, with some understandable asperity fueling his own response. 'I was watching men working on the killing beds, in the grinding and bone-cracking sheds and in the refrigerated cellars, where they stood in ice-cold water up to their ankles among frozen carcasses that hung like stalactites from the ceiling. It took more than a whiskey before dinner to obliterate the pitiful sounds that those hogs made when, shackled to the killing wheel by a hind leg, they squealed and grunted as they edged towards the company's big-muscled sticker, who knew how to use his long-handled throat-slitting knife.'

Walter also told me that, after spending a week in the fertilizer shed, no number of showers could get rid of the nauseating stench. 'It permeated every pore of my skin, every follicle in my hair. So maybe this explains why I never bothered to meet you last year, Robert — I stank!'

***

After the Second World War I continued my study of the Medici family at the American School in Rome. I didn't see much of Walter until I later landed a job at my old alma mater, the University of Chicago. And when I did see him after taking up my teaching position, he had by then closed the abattoir and was spending most of his time holding up the bar at the Arts Club.

On the few occasions that we met there for lunch, Walter regularly assured me that, on the matter of the family's art collection, everything was still proceeding according to his late mother's wishes. 'Father would bloody well turn in his grave if he could see the crap that I'm hanging in gallery,' Walter would tell me following a fourth Martini.

I was never invited to see Walter's latest acquisitions. But I was invited to meet his daughter, Jane. Born in 1947, just a few months before Walter's wife was killed in a car crash, Jane Henley went on to a finishing school in Switzerland then embarked on an undergraduate degree at the University of London. 'She's got her grandfather's collecting bug, loves Picasso's work and is probably spending more of her time in London's sales rooms and auction houses than in the library of that expensive university I'm paying for,' Walter assured me in mock exasperation. 'I'm not complaining. Jane's only making up for my lack of enthusiasm.'

It must have been towards the end of the 1960s that Walter brought his daughter to the club. Jane Henley turned out to be unattractive and painfully thin. For the daughter of a multi-millionaire, she was poorly dressed. She gave me the impression of being overly deferential to her father until, towards the end of the meal, she revealed that she'd just seen an exhibition of Picasso's sculptures in New York. Knowing that I was one of the few people in town who knew what her grandparents had begun collecting since 1901, this wiry unimposing young woman let loose.

'Are either of you aware that Picasso's sculptures are among the most playful, somber, whimsical and imaginative works that he ever produced?' Walter and I both shrugged our shoulders, then continued to listen. Jane Henley told us how Picasso had moved with natural ease from bronze-casting to wood-carving and from welding to modeling in clay. She hinted at the debt the younger generation of sculptors like David Smith, Louise Bourgeois and even Alberto Giacometti owed to "the Master". Then, focusing her piercing blue eyes in my direction and addressing me for the first time, she added: 'Professor Cunliffe, do you realize that the Henley collection doesn't include one sculpture by Picasso?'

I was genuinely impressed with Jane Henley's enthusiasm and offered her encouragement. Also, I naturally hoped that, now that she was back in Chicago, she would likewise encourage her father to open the doors of the family's collection to her fellow citizens. But Walter's daughter had evidently got enough from our encounter. After that first meeting, she vanished as abruptly as she had appeared.

Indeed, when I met Walter for lunch a few weeks later, I was not surprised to learn that Jane had moved back to Europe. 'She's spending my money buying every sculpture by Picasso that comes on to the market. I'll keep you posted!'

I never learned from him how successful Jane Henley had been. Instead, a few months later, I saw the Arts Club flag at half-mast. Walter had succumbed to cancer. Or perhaps to the booze. Or maybe from the exhaustion of collecting and caring for paintings that he didn't particularly like, couldn't sell and couldn't share with anyone but his daughter.

Walter Henley's early demise prompted renewed speculation about the fate of the collection. Had he made arrangements to bequeath whatever that glass-roofed building contained to the art museum? Rumor had it that his will revealed little, beyond the fact that everything now depended on the plans — or whims — of his sole heir, Jane Henley.

***

When I saw Walter's daughter again it was the late 1980s. By this time my parents had died and I had taken possession of the family home. I'd never lost interest in Picasso. Or forgotten that summer job during which I had come to know Mrs Charlotte Henley. In fact, I measured every other woman I met after that against her. None of them possessed Charlotte Henley's exuberance, her enthusiasm and her intelligence. Unwillingly stubborn to settle for second-best, I'd remained a bachelor. I was content. I ate well, for I had retained the family's chef. I took one long vacation a year. And I had my work.

I'd spent the last forty years of my academic career on one subject. Every couple of years I'd produced an article on the Medici family in order to remind the world that Professor Robert Cunliffe was still one of the world's experts in his field. But, without the much-promised book, my authority was diminishing so in 1988, I tried to do something about this. I took early retirement. And I made one last research trip to Italy. As it turned out, the trip was a success. I'd discovered new material on the Medici family in an obscure archive in Florence. I was riding high, anticipating the quick completion of my book.

My decision to spend a couple of weeks in Paris on my return to Chicago was not just a whim. In 1966, the French government had introduced a new tax law. Collectors could now avoid paying inheritance tax by donating their art to the French state. I'd read somewhere that the members of Picasso's fractured family were among the first to take advantage of this new law. Indeed, the state found a permanent home for the family's collection in the Marais district of Paris. And in 1986, the Musée Picasso duly came into being.

When I learned that Picasso's work was to be housed in a seventeenth century palace less than a mile from the high-tech iconoclastic Centre Georges Pompidou devoted to modern art, it seemed like an anachronistic venue for the twentieth century's leading avant-garde painter. But when I visited the Musée Picasso in the summer of 1989, I discovered that the French government could not have found a better place.

A baroque staircase led visitors to the first floor where a series of small-sized rooms avoided the necessity of installing temporary partitions. Floor-to-ceiling windows bathed the paintings and drawings in natural light. This made the canvases look as fresh as the day that Picasso had removed them from the easel and placed them against the wall of his studio to dry.

It was when I reached the first floor, devoted to Picasso's realistic oeuvre, that I found myself in for a surprise. There was certainly plenty of it, with two-dozen or so paintings and drawings from the estate of the feuding members of the Picasso family. But what astounded me was that the majority of work on display came from the Henley collection. I was uniquely qualified to vouch for this because thirty-five years earlier I'd recorded or hung almost every work that I now saw before me.

I was puzzled. The legal terms governing ownership of the Henley art collection had stipulated that it could never be sold during the current heir's lifetime. So, why were these pictures here? Had Jane Henley perhaps died young, like her father before her? And if not, why had she broken the terms of her grandfather's will? As the only other person privy to the contents of the Henley's palatial art gallery for so many years, I felt somewhat rueful. Because, if Jane Henley was still living, why hadn't she bothered to inform me about the collection's fate?

It was with mixed feelings that I made my way through the rest of the gallery. When I came to the top floor which featured Picasso's last work, the rooms were remarkably small. The paintings were hung cheek-by-jowl, as if jostling for space. They were poorly lit. The colors appeared drab and lifeless in that mellow light. And there was something more disconcerting about the work that made me feel uneasy. The brush strokes in virtually every painting, moved in one direction: from the top of the canvas to the bottom. That downward stroke of the brush seemed to announce that Picasso had come to the end of his creative life.

***

Few people on the day I visited the Musée Picasso had bothered climbing to the top floor to view these sad and tired paintings. In fact, there appeared to be only one other person there.

I recognized her at once. Her face bore the no-nonsense expression that precluded small talk, familiarity, let alone any warmth or intimacy. I didn't know whether she had recognized me. But when she had finished contemplating the last work in the room and was making her way towards the stairs leading to the lower floors, Jane Henley turned towards me and, in her own good time, asked: 'Are you free for dinner?'

We met in one of those small restaurants in the Marais where the ambience is more promising than the food. On closer observation, Jane certainly looked older, but she possessed that same bearing that had made it difficult for me to establish any connection with her on our previous meeting.

Before I had ordered the wine, Jane looked at me in that frighteningly focused manner so characteristic of her younger self and revealed that after Picasso's death in 1973 the market was flooded with his work. 'I had a field day, filling in the gaps of grandfather's collection and I even managed to acquire several sculptures.'

But, as Jane continued her story, it was clear that these halcyon days for private collectors had been short-lived. More and more corporations started investing in art. After the revaluation of the yen in 1985 the Japanese jumped into the art collecting game too. 'Suddenly,' Jane continued, 'there were fewer blue-chip Picassos on the market that I could afford. And the works that were within my means came with highly dubious "guaranteed authentic" and "original Picasso" labels.'

Before Walter Henley's death Jane revealed that her father had paid good prices for several so-called "masterpieces" and outright fakes. 'And so,' Jane briskly explained, 'I weeded out these inferior works, built a large bonfire at the back of the property down by the lake and burned the lot.'

'Are you telling me that you destroyed some of Picasso's work?' I asked, only to meet with the composed reply:

'Do you think that my grandparents would have wanted the collection to be tainted by inferior work, let alone by fakes?'

I refrained from telling Jane that what she might have found to be inferior another art collector or gallery owner or art historian might have viewed as significant. I refrained from reminding Jane Henley that neither she, nor her grandparents, nor her father nor any other art collector, including my beloved Medicis, ever owned the paintings, drawings and sculptures in their possession. They were simply the caretakers because if the work they collected was any good, it would outlive them.

'Anyway,' Jane continued, 'since I could no longer afford to expand the Henley collection, I decided to get rid of it.' I naturally asked her how she had got around Arthur Henley's express wishes that the collection should never be sold. 'I didn't *sell* the collection,' she almost shouted. 'I *gave* it away on the condition that the owners agreed to keep the name of the donor anonymous. So, you see, I have kept faith with the wishes of my grandparents: the donors will not only remain anonymous, the collection will continue to grow as other collectors donate their Picassos to the Musée Picasso.' And, she added with that wicked Charlotte Henley smile I so well remembered, 'I've got the satisfaction of watching the collection grow without being responsible for its upkeep.'

I could see a logic in this. 'So that's why you've bought an apartment within walking distance of the museum!'

'Not really. I'm about to sell it and move back to North America. That's where the most exciting work is being done now. In fact, there's a female artist in Vancouver whose work I've been tracking since she left art school a year ago…'

'And you're collecting some of her work.'

'Everything I can get my hands on before the prices soar. I can tell you, Professor Cunliffe,' she added, 'you'd be amazed to see how wonderful the eight by ten-foot canvases I've already acquired look against the white walls of the old gallery.'

Yes, I thought, Jane's at the top of her game by being on the bottom rung of the collecting ladder. Suddenly I saw that she had taken the family's talent for inconspicuous consumption to a new level. She had clearly discarded the pleasure of owning Picasso's, with all the worldly prestige that this might have brought, in favor of possessing work by an unheralded artist.

'And the best thing of all,' she added as I picked up the bill for dinner, 'nobody but you knows, that I'm collecting them.'

Gang of Three

Ruth's husband had one of the most dangerous jobs at the lumber mill, which dominated this small town on the coast of British Columbia. He also had a mixed reputation among his younger colleagues. When it came to sizing up a piece of freshly cut lumber as it emerged from the cutting shed, then pulling it off the green chain and sorting it according to size and quality, no one showed more skill than Jim. But the sheer monotony of the job, combined with Jim's show-off nature, led him to take chances. This was no secret to those who worked with him. Nor to his wife. Ruth always breathed a sigh of relief when she heard Jim drop his steel-toed boots on the back porch, then shout, 'What's for dinner?'

Of course, the nimblest of the workers at the lumber mill could cut corners by walking over the moving rollers on the green chain's conveyor belt without turning off the machine, as regulations stipulated. But Jim was large and physically awkward. He was at least ten years older than his colleagues. And during one late afternoon session when he was getting tired and weary, thinking more about pulling in an hour's fishing before dinner than pulling another piece of lumber off the rollers, he showed that he was neither nimble nor quick.

As Jim walked across the moving conveyor belt, he missed his footing. Before his co-worker had a chance to stop the machine, Jim's right foot, then most of his left leg, was caught between the rollers. There was a moment's silence until Jim saw his left leg at the far end of the conveyor belt. That's when he emitted a cry that sounded like a wounded animal caught in a leg-hold trap. Everyone moved into action; the conveyor belt finally stopped; and the safety officer put enough pressure on the femoral artery at the top of Jim's leg to stop the bleeding until the ambulance team arrived.

Jim was left to deal with the consequences. The lumber company promised compensation and Jim's doctor promised that he'd be walking in a month's time. But then there came the squabbles about responsibility and compensation. The arguments were protracted and dispiriting. Yes, the lumber company had failed to put up warning signs. But Jim knew the regulations well enough: "Never walk over the moving conveyor belt". Then there was the difficulty of finding the right prosthetic for Jim's missing leg and disagreement among the doctors as to when it should be fitted.

Ruth's decision to devote all of her time to Jim's healing was the only certainty in the couple's life. Even so, Jim was adamant that his wife should devote part of every day to her own art, just as she had done in the years before the accident. He'd worked an extra shift one day a month in order to help his wife pay her share of the studio that she rented with two friends. Though he preferred watching *Hockey Night in Canada* to gathering driftwood from the beach for his wife's assemblages, he had never complained when Ruth asked him to help her. 'I can't help you collect driftwood from the beach now, Ruth, but I can manage on my own for a couple of hours a day so that you can join your arty friends.' He was secretly proud when he saw her "driftwood things" as he called them, displayed at the agricultural hall as part of an exhibition by "the Gang of Three".

***

It was Karen who had come up with the group's name. Enviably slim at sixty-five and still improbably blonde, she had arrived in British Columbia from Ontario with a large pension — and with an even larger alimony settlement. But her greatest asset was her thirty years of experience in one of Toronto's largest advertising firms. Some said that even though Karen might be the least talented artist among the three women, she was also the driving force in establishing their collective identity. 'We've had the Group of Seven, the Regina Five and the Painters Eleven, but Canada has never had a Gang of Three!' Betty and Ruth had seen the point, and that's what the three women had now been calling themselves for twelve years.

As Karen intended, the name had a cachet, a sense of style. The sobriquet set them apart from other local amateur artists who were trying to make a living from their work. It was Karen who had convinced the town's mayor and city councilors that, with a bit of know-how, they could make their small community the artistic center of Vancouver Island. The town's officials had listened, then they acted. They printed maps that located every artist's studio within a ten-mile radius of the town. They gave over a part of the agriculture hall to a newly established amateur art society and paid for a professional artist to come over from Vancouver to give its members lessons. They changed zoning laws so that an art shop and a tourist-attracting restaurant could open on the main drag. And, in order to accommodate the burgeoning tourist trade, they turned a blind eye when the town's residents opened unregistered B&Bs.

Convinced that there must be something magical about the town and its environs, artists came from other areas of the province. Yet there was nothing special about the landscape surrounding the small settlement; and nothing unique about the light either. Just like every other part of coastal British Columbia, the landscape absorbed the light. On the other side of the country, it was just the opposite: light bounced off the land and the water, as Jock Colville and his Magic Realist colleagues had long demonstrated in their sharply-focused paintings.

For whatever reasons, the knock-on effect from the local council's initiative paid off, at least initially. Suddenly it seemed that almost everyone in the community claimed to be an artist. Sheds and garages were turned into studios. Signs appeared at the end of every driveway, lane and farm track announcing that "original paintings" or "sculptures" were for sale. So the Gang of Three had clearly hit the right spot at the right time. They benefited more than any other art group from the advertising campaign. During the summer months, a steady stream of beach-weary tourists visited the Gang of Three's studio.

'Is it really worth the intrusion?' Karen asked, worried that she was responsible for letting the genie out of the bottle.

'You bet it is,' Ruth replied.

There was no turning back. The summer trade was brisk; and during the off-season it wasn't bad either. Passing travelers who spotted the Gang of Three sign on the highway, offering free coffee to anyone who wanted to break their journey, duly found their way to their barn studio at the edge of Mr Humphrey's farm. The net result was that Ruth, Betty and Karen had soon found that they could earn enough from their sales to cover their annual rent.

***

The Gang of Three had not survived for so many years because they were each cut from the same bolt of cloth. Surely as the wife of a mill worker Ruth would never have found herself socializing with a posh hippy from

Vancouver like Betty or a former advertising executive from eastern Canada like Karen.

Ruth's two daughters, themselves married at an early age, felt that their mother's time would be better served by looking after their young children. But, at forty-five, Ruth didn't feel like a professional grandmother — yet. Maybe there would come a time when she'd submit to giving all of her attention to her grandchildren and to indulging in the one-up-man-ship game played by overly proud grandparents that went with it. But right now, Ruth wanted to create things. To make people see the world through her eyes and in her own particular way. The urge to do this had been running through her mind, like a subterranean river, during the two decades when her children, her household duties and her working-class ethos had conspired to keep her from doing anything about it.

Karen had been different, with no creative urge apparent. Painting had become a diversion from the pain of being laid off just before she qualified for a full pension and from the humiliation of being abandoned by her husband after twenty-five years of marriage. Being a member of the Gang of Three had given her a segue into the seaside community that she now called home. And then there was an unexpected bonus. Forced to give more than a cursory look at her surroundings helped Karen adapt to Vancouver Island's dense vegetation and restless ocean.

When she had first met Betty and Ruth, Karen had often become sentimental about the landscape surrounding her parents' lakeside cottage on Georgian Bay in Northern Ontario. And she continued to feel a sense of nostalgia, until Ruth, the only Vancouver-Island-born person in the Gang of Three, put a stop to her mawkish reminiscences by bluntly interjecting: 'But what about all the bugs in Ontario?'

And it was Betty who now chipped in, 'Not to mention the ferocious storms that made the Group of Seven give their paintings titles like *Stormy Weather* and *Eye of the Storm* and, now that I think of it, *March Storm* for good measure!'

Karen simply grinned and nodded in agreement.

Of course, Betty had not joined the group to escape grandchildren duty because she didn't have any grandchildren. Nor, unlike Karen, did she need to belong to an art group in order to paint — in the way that people bought dogs so that they would take a walk. But after meeting Karen and Ruth at the agricultural hall, she had certainly painted more regularly and with greater urgency. She had also discovered that she had an aptitude for teaching. It was Betty who had come up with the idea that Karen paint on wet paper — a technique developed by an early twentieth century English watercolorist. And Betty who had suggested that Ruth create her sculptures from found objects on the beach right in front of her own home rather than trying to model a piece of clay. Betty also discovered that she had a great capacity for being a good friend and realized that hither to meeting Karen and Ruth she had been lonely, had lacked conversation and company. It was not surprising that Betty came to the studio more frequently than her two friends.

However socially and economically diverse, Betty, Karen and Ruth nonetheless shared one trait: a strong sense of their own significance as artists and a feeling of mutual esteem. They were unafraid to hand out unfavorable comments to their amateur competitors when they viewed their work at the local art shows. They felt equally free to criticize the professional artists whose work they viewed on their twice-yearly visits to Vancouver.

When it came to discussing their own work, they took an altogether more constructive attitude. Betty's two colleagues encouraged her to practice the Hard-Edged style of abstract painting that she'd mastered at art school in the 1960s, even though it was now twenty-five years out of date. Karen's watercolor technique, which involved dropping large dabs of paint on to wet paper, was pronounced interesting, if enigmatic. And when it came to Ruth's frequently inelegant driftwood assemblages, Betty and Karen could always be relied upon to find symmetry and meaning in her constructions, albeit ones that might have escaped their creator — or anyone else who viewed Ruth's work.

***

Yet now, with their twelfth year upon them, they had a problem, as the demand for their work began to decline. It seemed that everyone in the town who could afford it had already bought at least one of the Gang of Three's works. Moreover, thanks to the mayor's successful marketing campaign, someone had built a café on the highway that gave wall space to members of the local art society. This was unwelcome competition in a shrinking market.

And there was something else: the Gang of Three had gone stale. They now felt that they had sketched every scenic location within an hour's drive of their ramshackle barn studio. They'd taken their sketchbooks up the side of the mountain that formed a back-drop to their small seaside settlement and captured the Gulf Islands, that peppered the Salish Sea. They'd duly pushed their way through waxy-leafed salal bushes and metallic-colored western sword ferns until they came to a clearing in the forest where they pretended to be the province's most famous painter, the long-dead Emily Carr. They'd set up their easels on two-mile-long pebbly beaches. They'd painted the weather-silvered planks of a long-deserted fish cannery on the outskirts of town.

They badly needed a new theme, a new subject for their work. They were not prepared to flex their artistic muscles merely for art's sake. Or for a quick sale. And they couldn't risk alienating their loyal, largely conservative and well-heeled clientele. So far, the Gang of Three had managed to please everyone: the people who bought their art, Mr Humphrey who rented them his derelict barn and Canada Revenue who allowed them to deduct the studio rental and art supplies on their tax returns.

When the rains began in late November, the Gang of Three had looked elsewhere for inspiration and sought to turn one another's pets, their friends, and one another, into works of art. None of it really worked. On one occasion the three artists had thrown all subject matter out of the door and created work from their imagination. Ruth called the results free-fall art. It had been an interesting experiment, for them at least, but it had not led anywhere, certainly not in promoting sales of their work. They were now desperate for inspiration.

No wonder Ruth and Karen listened to Betty when she came up with a new suggestion. Unlike them, their friend came from what used to be called a "good" family, one that could afford to send their daughter to a posh private school then financed their daughter's studies at Vancouver's leading art school. But while Betty had walked away with all the prizes after three years of study and been invited to join the city's leading private art gallery, her promising career had gone nowhere. After leaving art school she had become pregnant. And her situation hadn't improved when, just after the birth of her child, Betty's drug-obsessed partner left her with a son and a large mortgage. That's when she had turned her back on the province's largest city — and on all the opportunities it offered a budding artist. She had crossed the Salish Sea to Vancouver Island, moved into a wartime bungalow on the edge of a small coastal town and, with the help of her parents and a part-time job as a cashier at the local supermarket, put her son Kurt through school and university.

It didn't matter to Ruth and Karen that Betty had never become a professional artist. It hadn't stopped them from admiring their friend's technical ability, her knowledge of art history and, above all, her dedication to her art. For Betty had never stopped painting, even when it had meant doing so on the kitchen table, between shifts of working at the supermarket and caring for her son. And had never stopped trying to take her work in a new direction. What Betty now proposed to them was that, in their quest for inspiration, they look no further than their own paint-splattered table, covered with its water-filled milk bottles, their used paint brushes, the empty tubes of acrylic paint and tins of glue. 'Let's create a still life from this stuff and see what we can come up with in half an hour.'

It's not as though these women were about to do something new, as Betty readily acknowledged. The ancient Egyptians had indeed decorated the walls of their funerary tombs with images of fish, grain and meat; artists working in the first century AD had painted frescoes displaying the culinary abundance of Pompeii's wealthy residents. Betty had often described the meticulously rendered oil paintings that Dutch artists had produced during the seventeenth century. It was during what became known as the Golden Age of Dutch art, that still life painting became high art, with artists celebrating the prosperity of their citizens and the transience of their lives. Betty had also told Karen and Ruth how artists from Van Gogh and Cezanne to Picasso had used still life as a vehicle for exploring modernist ideas.

The two women listened intently to Betty. They could see that the haphazard array of items that jostled for space on their studio worktable might offer The Gang of Three an opportunity to do something different. Betty moved the paraphernalia back and forth, on and off the table, until everyone was satisfied with the composition. It was now eleven-twenty a.m. and Karen set the old-fashioned alarm clock to ring at noon. 'If we begin in ten minutes, we'll be able to discuss the results of our work over lunch.'

Betty attached a four-by-four-foot canvas to her convertible easel and laid several tubes of acrylic paint on a nearby table. While she was doing this, Karen transferred a piece of Japanese rag paper from a bucket of water on to a pane of glass. Then she opened her box of watercolor cakes and placed her long-handled, sable-tipped brushes into several jars of water. Ruth dragged various-sized pieces of driftwood from the storage shed into the studio. Like hundred-meter sprinters crouched at the starting blocks, Betty, Karen and Ruth waited for the big hand to reach the bottom of the clock at 11.30.

When the alarm bell rang half an hour later, Betty and Karen put down their paint brushes and Ruth dropped the piece of driftwood that she had been desperately trying to attach to three other pieces of wood. Hungrily, the women grabbed their large handbags — for all female artists carry over-sized handbags — and dug out their sandwiches. Ruth poured everyone a cup of coffee from a battered thermos. Then, balancing their bottoms on portable sketching stools and their sandwiches on their laps, they put their coffee mugs on the floor and considered one another's efforts.

It was not surprising that each of them had approached this challenge in a distinctive manner. Predictably, Betty's canvas of the still life set-up consisted of several horizontal bands of primary color kept four inches apart. 'It makes me think of Rothko,' Karen said naively as she examined the painting, even though Betty knew that she would have been closer to the mark if she'd compared her work to Frank Stella.

Karen's colleagues judged her own depiction of the bottles and paint cans as a faithful, though highly impressionistic interpretation of the still life assemblage. And although Ruth's driftwood sculpture had no apparent relationship to the subject at hand, her friends pronounced it as mysterious, hinting at dimensions that a perceptive observer was left to discern. 'It forces us to use our imagination,' Betty said as Ruth made a final, desperate attempt to glue her sculpture together.

Like almost every other session before it in previous years, this one ended with mutual admiration and reciprocal praise. Each of the three women returned home with the assurance that she had produced a suitable entry for the up-coming show.

As usual, the spring fair at the agricultural hall opened on May Day. The painting section, located at the back of the hall, had to compete for attention with handicraft, baking, flower arranging and wood-turning exhibits. And, of course, Betty, Karen and Ruth had to compete with their fellow artists. This year they had chosen to do this by exhibiting their work under a banner: "The Gang of Three Creates Art — in just half an hour!"

Curious to see what artists could accomplish in so short a time, people gathered around their display. Those who might have bought their first painting or sculpture from the Gang and others who might have added another piece to their collection were united in their lack of enthusiasm. Indeed, everyone who viewed the work agreed that the business of creating a painting or sculpture in thirty minutes was nothing more than an attention-getting gimmick. 'My dog could do that if I put a paintbrush in his mug,' one discouraged viewer said within hearing distance of Betty.

'Don't worry,' Karen said as they dismantled their banner and packed up their work at the end of the day, 'we've got the summer tourist trade ahead of us.'

'But this is the first time that we haven't sold a thing at the May Day Fair,' Ruth noted with abject realism.

'Come on girls...' Karen began brightly in a determined effort to find something encouraging to say, but found that she was unable to complete her sentence.

Predictably, the Gang of Three did make a few sales over the summer months, but their sense of malaise persisted. Betty continued to roll bands of primary color on to an unprimed canvas. But she was unable to achieve the zen-like trance that made her body weightless and that took her to another place. Instead, she encountered frustration at not being able to express her surroundings through her art.

Karen continued to put dabs of watercolor on to wet paper but the colors ran together forming a brown sludge. Now established in the community through her membership in the Gang of Three, she began to wonder whether the group had served its purpose and whether another venture might better occupy her time in future.

Ruth was less concerned with her inability to avoid making her driftwood assemblages look like a pile of pick-up-sticks. Sensing her friends' dissatisfaction with their own work, she feared that the studio sessions that released her from grandmother duties and gave her a life of her own were coming to an end.

Though no one uttered a word of discouragement, their unease continued. They did not acknowledge boredom from uninspired repetition. They did not express fear of being unable to sell their work and thus failing to come up with the rent of their barn studio. And none of them hinted at no longer enjoying one another's company. Yet a sense that the Gang of Three's days might be numbered now hung in the air. Then, just before the ninth decade of the twentieth century began, Ruth's husband Jim lost his left leg.

***

In the most literal sense, Ruth's husband had been forced to hang up his boots. No one knew why Jim wanted to keep the pair that he had worn on that fateful day. Or why he wanted them hung, like an unlucky talisman, on a hook in the back porch. Ruth avoided the boots by using the front door entrance of their log cabin, until Jim asked why she wasn't entering the building through the back door. Not wanting an argument, she packed up the boots and took them to the barn studio where they remained until, in a fit of cleaning to ease the boredom of her work, Betty found them in a cardboard box.

Betty knew that boots and shoes had provided a subject for one of her favorite artists. Vincent van Gogh had made a habit of buying second-hand working men's boots and shoes in the Paris flea-market. If they didn't look sufficiently used, he'd put them on and walk through mud puddles, in the rain. Scholars differ as to why the Dutch artist found worn-out boots to be a worthy subject for his art. Some say that they represented the hard, yet picturesque life of the working man. More psychologically minded scholars suggested that they were a metaphor for the hardships that van Gogh himself had suffered during his years in Paris.

Betty also knew that Ruth was suffering, that she was almost as traumatized by the accident as her husband. Ruth never talked about the phantom pain in Jim's missing leg that made him insist that the limb was still there. 'No, it's gone, Jim,' Ruth told him when he woke her up in the middle of the night screaming. Nor, during her two-hour visits to the studio, did Ruth mention Jim's debilitating fatigue or the doctor's concern about the possibility of infection or deep vein thrombosis. Nor did she complain that Jim's horrific injury had reduced them to living on an income just above the minimum wage.

'We've got to do something to help Ruth come to grips with this heart-breaking situation,' Karen told Betty one day, just before their colleague arrived for her morning session. 'Let's begin by taking over her share of the studio rent.' Betty responded with an appreciative nod, then she placed a large cardboard box on the paint-stained table. She had another idea of how she and Karen could help their friend.

Jim's boots didn't need distressing like a mock piece of peasant furniture or dragged through mud puddles in order to make them a suitable subject to paint. They were already scuffed. They were already cracked just below the steel-plated toe cap. They smelled. And, they had a further telling feature — they were blood-stained.

If Karen was shocked by Betty's new still life set up, then Ruth was doubly so. Yet she didn't reveal her mixed feelings when, upon entering the studio, she saw Jim's boots on the paint-stained table. Instead, she took a large piece of Karen's Japanese rag paper and a stub of black charcoal and, much to the surprise of her colleagues, Ruth began to draw. The result was an impression rather than a realistic rendering of the subject before her. Art historians might claim that the drawing's thick angular lines were reminiscent of the work created by the German Expressionists following the First World War. But when Betty and Karen examined the results, they didn't think of German Expressionism or any other art movement to which Ruth's drawing might be compared. For them, it wasn't how Ruth had captured Jim's boots in her charcoal drawing that mattered. It was the catharsis, the sort of purification that had come from the act, the doing, the execution of the charcoal drawing.

'She never tells us how she's coping,' Karen exclaimed after Ruth left the studio barn, having put in her two hours.

'That's right,' Betty agreed, as she, too, examined her colleague's charcoal drawing. 'But Ruth doesn't have to say a thing,' she continued. 'The tragedy, the stress and the uncertainty that dominate her life are all here.'

The boots remained on the table for two weeks. And when Ruth sensed that her colleagues had become tired of drawing them, she suggested how they could be used in another way. 'Why don't we mount an exhibition around Jim's boots?'

Betty immediately agreed. She made arrangements to take a photograph of the green chain and blow it up to life size. Karen, who was equally enthusiastic, offered to obtain a recording of the machinery. Using her old contacts at the National Film Board of Canada she poached the soundtrack of a recent documentary featuring British Columbia's logging industry. Indeed, once the women had decided to pool their efforts, the project expanded. Karen contacted the compensation board and got a copy of the rules, which should have been posted, but did not appear in any of the photographs that Betty had taken inside the mill. She also obtained portraits — God only knows how — of the lumber company's president and every member of the compensation board. All of these images were enlarged; some of them were even framed.

Ruth was left to make further large-scale drawings of Jim's boots. More remarkably, she managed to persuade Jim himself to allow her to record his experience of the accident and its tragic aftermath. And when everything had been assembled, Karen sweet-talked the mayor and the town's council members into giving over the community hall for a special exhibition. It was a due mark of their feelings of sympathy towards Jim and Ruth that the officials all agreed. 'It'll boost the tourist trade during a slack time of year,' the mayor argued when he presented the Gang of Three's project to the local council, 'and maybe improve our relations with the local logging company.'

The Gang of Three's installation made different kinds of appeal to those who became involved, not only to city officials, but members of the province's compensation board, representatives of the lumber company and the many men and women who had themselves worked at the mill. None of them knew quite what they were in for when, clutching their invitations, they entered the Gang of Three's special exhibition on a rainy day in November 1990. Some saw photographs of their workplace; a few of them saw larger-than-life images of themselves. Everyone heard the clang, clang, clang of the green chain, broadcast from a large speaker at the corner of the hall. Many were moved as they listened to the recording of Jim's voice recounting the tragic accident. And they all saw the blood-stained workman's boots, sitting on a paint-stained table in the center of the agricultural hall.

***

'I've had requests to borrow our exhibition from almost every public and private gallery in the country,' Karen declared a week after the Gang of Three's installation had received nationwide coverage in the press.

'Well,' Betty added with a grimace, 'I've had threats from the lumber company and a discouraging letter from the mayor who advises us to avoid mounting our exhibition in another city.'

Both women looked towards Ruth, who obviously had news of her own.

'Jim has just had a letter from the compensation board — they're going to reconsider his case.'

However, you looked at it, the project had been an attraction-getting success, for it had certainly not been ignored. It had helped Jim himself in tangible ways, in regard to both recuperation and possibly compensation too. It had helped reconcile Ruth to a tragedy that she could now almost cope with, not least by getting back to work as an artist and by having the support of her two friends. It had certainly put the Gang of Three on the cultural map by drawing attention to their work from far outside their locality.

'So where do we go from here?' Betty wondered as she unpacked a fresh box of acrylic paints a week after their exhibition had been dismantled. 'Should the Gang of Three now look for more good causes to support? Or would we be exploiting another human tragedy simply for the sake of our art?'

As though reading Betty's mind as to whether creating another installation would be a worthy activity, Karen simply said: 'I think that we should get back to our own work.' And their eyes naturally shifted to see the reaction of their fellow artist, the woman for whom the image of Jim's boots was inevitably laden with more significance than just as a subject for their art. Ruth paused for a moment before she looked up at her two friends. 'If one of you can help me gather some driftwood from the beach,' she said as she glanced towards her friends, 'I'm on.'

Double Bluff

I met him over croissants and café-au-lait a few weeks after he had arrived in Paris. It was obvious enough that we were both foreigners, not least of all to each other. 'I'm Charles Davenport, how-do you-do,' I said, conventionally enough, as I proffered a hand across the table. My breakfast companion grasped my hand and, in over-familiar American fashion said, 'Pleased to meet you, Charlie, I'm Bud Hardy.'

We were both living in the sort of respectable but down-at-heel hotel where the women ate their breakfasts in floral-patterned dressing gowns and the concierge turned a blind eye to unauthorised night-time visitors. I'd been in Paris for a year and was attempting to turn myself into a writer. I'd even produced a draft of my first novel, though I have to admit that I was growing increasingly bored with the results. In fact, all I had managed to do during my year abroad, was to put myself on the other side of the English Channel — thus avoiding my father's wish that I follow him into law — and to catch a glimpse of Simone de Beauvoir at the Café de Flore. Any chance of getting to know this unremarkable-looking woman, with that trademark bandana covering her unwashed hair and the famous

French shrug that she gave to anyone who approached her table, was as improbable as passing my bar exams or publishing a best-selling novel.

After meeting Bud Hardy, however, it didn't take me long to discover that, when it came to telling a tale, I had met my match. When my new American acquaintance was talking, I found that I got drawn into his stories, almost against my will, as I sat listening while the plot uncoiled, from predictable to probable, from likely to surprising but always with a mesmerising thread of plausibility to tie up the loose ends. Only afterwards did I wonder if some parts were actually true.

***

Almost every American I had met in Paris insisted on telling me their life story within a few minutes of our acquaintance. I wondered if it was a way of getting me to tell mine. A way to level the playing field, which could only be accomplished if they knew their opponent well. Predictably, Bud was less interested in hearing about me than in talking about himself. Thus, within a few days, I learned that Bud Hardy not only came from California but from the most glamorous part of it: Hollywood. Two generations of his family had lived off tinsel town. His father, Gerald Hardy, was a mortician who liked to boast that he had not only improved the faces of many a star before their final appearance, he'd been the last to see them before bolting down the lids of their gold trimmed coffins. Bud's younger brother, Jack, wanted to become an actor. Though well-built and handsome in a sort of rugged way, he failed every screen test that he took. Alas, the only job Jack could land was as a stunt man. At first Jack made good, turning weedy unexercised actors into muscular hulks, until, as Bud Hardy revealed, one stunt too many saw his brother to an early death.

Bud made it clear that he had more talent than his younger brother and more charm than his po-faced father. A born salesman, he'd begun young by licking the chalky liquorish coating off a jawbreaker, then selling the transformed sweet to his classmates for twice the price. Most kids didn't have the patience to suck the white jawbreaker to the end, so bought another. Those who did and discovered the bitter-tasting aniseed at the centre of the candy, knew they had been fooled. But they never retaliated. 'I was always the largest boy in the class,' Bud proclaimed and I didn't press him any further.

On graduating from high school, so Bud told me, he had turned his entrepreneurial skills in various directions. He came up with the idea of manufacturing edible underwear. Panties and bras would be produced in the popular flavours of the day: tutti-frutti, cream soda and lemon-lime. However, the project never got off the ground because whatever people said about carefree, risqué Hollywood, there was a conservative streak running up and down Sunset Boulevard and

Mulholland Drive that prevented anyone from investing in Bud's scheme. Desperate for success, Bud tried his hand at photography.

At first, he took candid shots with a polaroid camera. 'But nobody wanted to wait the fifteen minutes that it took my camera to develop the film.' So, he found people who were willing to wait. This is when Bud revealed that he had entered his father's mortuary after hours, unbolted the lids of the coffins and photographed the stars. Before he had a chance to market these underground photographs, Gerald Hardy caught his son in the act. Forced to leave home, Bud put his tail between his legs and moved further south to San Diego. 'This is when I became an art dealer, Charlie.'

Bud Hardy knew that velvet paintings were tacky and flashy: 'No wonder some people call them crap,' he told me one morning. It was clear that Bud also knew — somewhere at the back of his mind — that the Mexican artists who produced them were poorly paid and that inhaling the black leather dyes used to outline their cartoon images could clog up their lungs. Sure, velvet paintings had a bad reputation, went Bud's line of thinking. Sure, they were the kind of pictures that the art world loved to hate. 'But this didn't stop me from making an honest living by selling them.'

I could just imagine Bud Hardy dressed in the off-white linen suit that he'd worn when I first met him. Proudly declaring that he was no door-to-door salesman, Bud had set up four bi-fold screens on which he displayed the "paintings", on alternate days, in the lobbies of San Diego's black and white only Douglas Hotel and Creole Palace. His clientele were sailors attached to the Pacific Fleet, travelling salesmen, housewives, whatever. They were of all tastes and colours. But all of them had one thing in common: they liked the way the subjects in the paintings, ranging from poker-playing cats and South Sea hula dancers to Spanish bullfighters and bronco-busting cowboys, leapt out of the coal-black velvet background. They saw the chance of owning an original work of art. And, above all, at the price Bud Hardy was asking, most of his clients could afford to buy one or two.

Of course, Bud Hardy boasted that he had paid far less for the work. 'Even so,' he insisted, 'the five-hundred-per-cent mark-up that I slapped onto every painting that I sold never made me a wealthy man.' Nevertheless, he added, 'Providing I worked a twelve-hour day, I earned a regular, comfortable, get-by living and was even able to put a little aside. Until about 1950, that is.'

That's when the market, year by year, became flooded with do-it-yourself, paint-by-number kits and copper handicraft sets. 'Suddenly everyone thought that they were a goddamn artist,' Bud complained. I could just imagine the results hanging on the walls of hundreds of prefabricated office buildings and bungalows that had been built across America following the Second World War.

In the good years, Bud claimed that he could sell one of his velvet paintings for the price of two bottles of Kentucky's finest bourbon. By the late 1950s, however, the cost of a velvet painting was equivalent to one bottle of vodka. Pleading market conditions, he persuaded his Mexican-based artists to accept less for their life-threatening efforts. He likewise proposed a reduction in the commissions due to the Creole Palace and Douglas Hotel. Unwilling to accept Bud's new offer, the hotels denied him exhibition space in their lobbies. Devastated, Bud Hardy saw that this was the end of the road for his old trade and his old way of life.

However, my new acquaintance was nothing if not resourceful; a man full of bright ideas; a man who was ready to use his fertile imagination in refashioning himself and his ambitions. So, I was not surprised to learn that this was when Bud packed up his bi-fold screens and put them, along with the residue of his stock and all his worldly goods — which didn't amount to much — into a lock-up storage facility. He withdrew his life savings — which were similarly meagre — from the Bank of America. And he changed continents.

***

Bud Hardy's life story was told to me in a disjointed fashion, piece by piece, bit by bit, episode by episode, revelation after revelation. Thus, it was no surprise when, on the second week of our acquaintance, he revealed that he had come to Paris to see *original* paintings. He had certainly acquired the kit for it. A beret sat like an up-turned saucer on his balding head. A loosely fitting zoot suit — obviously new — cloaked his large ungainly figure. And a briar pipe, that was more of a prop than a pacifier, completed his attire. The only thing that was out of place in Bud Hardy's attempt to pass as a native Parisian was the large bulge that rose, like an unwanted boil, under the pocket of his jacket. 'I always keep a mickey of my favourite scotch close to my heart,' he announced as he patted his breast pocket and gave me a conspiratorial wink.

I liked Bud Hardy; but with some measure of English condescension, I assumed that this unsophisticated, crass and over-familiar American would quickly tire of looking at pictures. Or that, even before boredom or weariness set in, Bud Hardy would run out of money, don the crumpled linen business suit in which he'd arrived and return to the United States. However, I could not have been more wrong and my assumption that Bud Hardy did not possess one aesthetic bone in his body proved unwarranted. Only a few weeks after I'd met him, he came to breakfast clutching E.H. Gombrich's recently published *Story of Art* under his arm. 'I'm goanna spend six days a week at the "Loovera",' he announced as he balanced the book on the edge of the round table, 'and I'm not leaving the city until I've looked at every statue and painting in the building.'

Working one's way through the history of European art at the Louvre was a challenging prospect. It seemed an unlikely activity for a man who told me that he had spent the previous decade selling velvet paintings. But this tall and stooped Californian, whose enormous belly threated to topple him over when he shuffled into breakfast and whose age must have been double that of mine, proved that it was never too late to learn. Indeed, I had already sensed that Bud was a quick learner, ready to pick up new ideas, ready to improvise by putting information to good use. Day by day, breakfast after breakfast, I couldn't help but notice that the bookmark in Bud's copy of Gombrich's hefty tome was moving closer to the last page of the book.

I wondered if my new acquaintance could become a friend — someone I could introduce to the group of ex-pat North Americans with whom I hung out at the Café de Flore. I speculated whether Bud's exaggerated efforts to fit into a Bohemian Paris that had vanished with Ernest Hemingway's departure from the city in the 1920s, might be a bit too close to home for his fellow North Americans, might even mock their own pretensions. Maybe it was just as well, then, that I never seized the opportunity to draw Bud Hardy into my small circle of friends.

Indeed, after four months of sharing breakfast with me in the lobby of our shabby hotel, Bud suddenly disappeared. He had left no forwarding address. He had given no hint of further travel plans. He hadn't even said farewell. I assumed that he had run out of pictures and sculptures to study at the Louvre and had moved to another European capital in his pursuit of that elusive *original* European work of art. Within a few weeks I had forgotten about the strange American and was focussing on my own writing.

***

I published my first novel two years later in 1954 and the owner of Le Mistral bookstore, George Whitman, launched it for me. All of my friends from the Café de Flore were there to help me celebrate, for I was the first among our small group of wannabe writers to actually publish a book. Much to my surprise, during the course of the evening they all behaved. None of them spilled their wine and made the wooden floor sticky; still less did they pocket any of the books that were stacked on the bookshelves and tables within the store and on the stands at front of the shop. My father, having given up hope that I would return to university, qualify as a lawyer and join his firm, came over from London. The attendance was sufficiently large, then, to save me from embarrassment. And, since everyone purchased at least one copy of my novel, Le Mistral bookstore covered the cost of providing cheap red wine and paltry hors d'oeuvres.

Feeling truly launched as a writer, I was in my element. I had signed more than sixty copies of my book.

I had heard my father tell everyone in the bookshop that I was his son. And, at a late point in the evening George Whitman had taken me aside and offered to host another event, should I publish a second novel. The bookstore owner was in fact in the process of doing this, when into the bookshop walked Bud Hardy.

He was a changed man. The beret, the zoot suit and the pipe had gone, along with the stoop; and so too had the bulge under his breast pocket. 'I'm Armand now,' Bud quickly whispered when I made moves to introduce him to the other guests. 'Remember, Charlie, I'm Armand — Armand, Armand!'

I got the point. Armand he was, as his new lifestyle affirmed. For no one called Bud, as I learned in the next few minutes, would be a permanent resident at the Hôtel Ritz; or dine three times a week at La Tour D'Argent; or wear handmade suits by Cifonelli, with their famous Milan-style buttonholes, step collars and cigarette sleeves. Still less would the old Bud Hardy carry a silver-knobbed walking stick that now transformed him into the likeness of the Ballet Russe's famous impresario, Serge Diaghilev (minus only the top hat and white streak of hair that had raced from Diaghilev's forehead to his crown).

It was thus Armand who bought five copies of my book. It was Armand who charmed the other guests, including even my father, a man who rarely hid his antipathy to anyone who wasn't born and educated in England. And at the end of the evening, it was Armand who invited me to join him for a celebratory dinner at one of Paris's finest restaurants, La Tour D'Argent.

I had never expected to meet up with Bud Hardy again — and in a sense I never did. For Bud belonged in my memory to that shabby hotel with its round breakfast tables crowded with cups of café au lait and croissants, with its small metal chairs that threatened to collapse under the weight of its heaviest customers and with those overly-made-up women who came to breakfast wrapped in their garishly coloured dressing gowns.

But at La Tour D'Argent the following day, it was Armand with whom I shared dinner. And what a meal it was. We ate prawns from Dublin. We toyed with truffle foie gras. We sampled wild pike dumplings accompanied by yellow and red nasturtiums. We tasted perfectly aged Comté cheese and concluded with a chocolate, nougat and almond mousse. The waiters addressed my host as "Monsieur Armand" and, expectant of a generous tip, hovered over our table, like vultures around new kill.

I ate too much and drank far too much wine. And for once it was me, not Bud, who did most of the talking. I had already begun writing my second novel and was too green to realize that by repeatedly describing the plot and the characters to anyone who was willing to listen, I was in danger of talking myself out of completing the actual book. Although Bud, or rather Armand, was probably more interested in consuming the food than in listening to me, he nodded at the appropriate moments, making no effort to cut into my lengthy peroration. Indeed, it was only towards the end of the evening that it dawned upon me that I had not addressed one single question to my host.

Setting my British reserve aside, I belatedly asked Armand how he had transformed himself into a sophisticated European oozing with savoir-faire. For a moment, the old Bud emerged. He waved his wrist as though he was trying to swat a fly then patted his chest. Three waiters appeared at our table; then, sensing a false alarm, they vanished. A few minutes later, I made a second attempt to satisfy my curiosity. This time, more composed, it was Armand who waved his napkin with a flourish. The waiters reappeared carrying the bill on a gold-plated salver. The reunion dinner was over; it seemed as though another engagement prevented us from ending our sumptuous meal with a glass of cognac. My host rose from the table, grasped his cane and, within a few minutes, was stepping into a taxi. He left me standing on the curb of the Quai de la Tournelle.

There was little possibility that I'd bump into my old acquaintance a third time. Certainly not while we both remained in Paris. For one thing, Bud and I now moved in different circles. For another, I'd hardly been good company during our reunion dinner. In fact, I'd been a self-absorbed bore. Bud's new lifestyle would therefore remain a mystery to me until, a year after our dinner at La Tour D'Argent, I encountered a British school friend at the Louvre.

***

James Conway wasn't at Paris's most famous art gallery to view the paintings, but to copy them. I found him sitting on a small portable three-legged canvas-topped stool in front of the gallery's most celebrated painting: Leonardo Da Vinci's portrait of Francesco del Giocondo's wife, popularly known as Mona Lisa.

'This will be my fifth copy,' James boasted as he turned his delicately featured visage in my direction. 'And this time I'm going to get my copy as close as I can to the original.'

It seemed that copying masterpieces was part of the curriculum at the Académie des Beaux Arts where James was in his third year. Built on centuries of professional practice, copying was an art form that made immense demands on the student. As James assured me when we subsequently met for a drink at the Café de Flore, copying masterpieces in the Louvre had helped him to see. It had introduced him to a variety of brushstrokes, textures and drying oils. And it had certainly taught him patience: James had learned how to wait for the oil paint to dry before adding another stroke of the brush.

'And before you ask me if what I'm doing is above board, Charles,' he concluded his disquisition on the merits of copying masterpieces, 'remember that no fewer than eight of Da Vinci's contemporaries made their own copies of the master's most famous painting. In any case, if I wanted to *forge* the Mona Lisa, I'd paint on a wooden panel rather than on a canvas and I'd use egg-tempera rather than oil-based paints.'

Perhaps James seemed just a little too insistent on making his point, telling me more than once that, 'Just like Leonardo's own friends and generations of art students after them, I'm not forging, I'm simply copying.'

***

In due course, I learned more. To put it unkindly, I discovered that James was not just fulfilling his obligations as a student at the Académie des Beaux Arts by producing a reasonable facsimile of Da Vinci's famous painting. He had become the monkey performing tricks for an organ grinder. James did what he was told — he'd produced five copies of the Mona Lisa by the time I met him — and applied what he had learned. And whatever his own suspicions about what happened to the copies that he painstakingly executed, once he had sold them to Monsieur Armand — the organ-grinder himself — James had asked no further questions.

I would only hear the full story — if it really was the full story — from Bud Hardy himself when we indeed met for a third time many years later. On this occasion, he wasn't walking in or out of La Tour D'Argent restaurant, or wearing a suit made by Cifonelli or carrying a silver-knobbed walking stick. Bud was wearing the crumpled linen business suit that he'd worn in Paris so long ago. As I had not predicted when I first met him, Bud was now living in California under circumstances that I would never have imagined possible.

He had bought a house situated between the coastal mountains and San Diego Bay in Del Mar Heights and was living there in splendour off his earnings from his golden years in Paris. By this time, he felt free to spill the beans.

Bud remembered my school friend James well but hadn't been interested in the frisson that the art student claimed to have gotten from replicating and thereby demystifying, or taking possession of, a great work of art by copying it. Bud had been interested in something else.

Unexpectedly, but irresistibly, Bud's old entrepreneurial instincts had been aroused when, walking through the Louvre palace, he had encountered students copying well known masterpieces. He had found that his attention became focused on what he could do with the finished product. He came to appreciate that the aesthetic value of the students' copies far surpassed that of the velvet paintings now mouldering in an abandoned lock-up facility halfway around the world. And he appreciated, above all, that their financial value was of a wholly higher order. In short, within a year of arriving in Paris, Bud — or rather, Armand — had gone back into business.

In his Californian retirement, Bud Hardy told me that if a visitor to the Louvre had stood for more than thirty seconds in front of a painting, that was the moment for him to act — or rather for Monsieur Armand to launch into a well-rehearsed routine. It was Armand who would sidle up to the viewer then swing his silver-topped walking stick in order to gain attention. And when he got it, Armand would praise the viewer for focussing on one of the most important works in the Louvre. And when viewers gave him a quizzical look as if to ask, "we don't really know why we like this painting so much", Armand had been unfailingly happy to tell them why they did so. He had given a potted history, à la Gombrich, of the artist. He had recounted the unique circumstances under which the painting had been executed. And, drawing on the great art historian once again, he would compare the work to those produced by the artist's inferior contemporaries.

This raconteur was not simply relishing his own cleverness in those Paris days. Bud explained to me that, after his eloquent oration, Armand would intimate that he had the means to acquire an *original copy* — as he liked to call it — of the work itself.

Sure, most gallery-goers were initially affronted when Armand first approached them. After all, an art gallery was a place for meditation, for enlightenment and, more often than not, for assignations. It was a place where one whispered. Where one walked in slow motion at a sleepwalker's pace. Where one never approached a stranger. And where you didn't expect to see a man waving a silver-topped walking stick as though it was a town-crier's bell.

In retrospect, hearing Bud's story in California, it was all a great joke. But, as we both recalled, those were the days before the docents in art galleries imparted knowledge to small groups whom they shepherded from one painting to another. The days before uniformed officials sat on uncomfortable-looking chairs at the corner of every gallery in order to guard the works of art. Before large numbers of North Americans entered the Louvre with their degrees in fine arts, or their well-thumbed guidebooks and exhibition catalogues in hand. It was, above all, the days before the penchant to capture a work with a digital camera, rather than with the naked eye, made contemplating a picture on one's own for more than a few seconds impossible.

I already knew from James Conway how Monsieur Armand's patronage had enabled him and many of his fellow students to move out of their garrets, to eat decent food and to travel around Europe during their summer vacation. I had heard how Monsieur Armand would treat James to a meal (though I suspected that it was not at La Tour D'Argent), and how this worldly man who possessed a knowledge of art that James himself was just beginning to acquire would now invite him to the Hôtel Ritz, where their transactions were usually made over a drink in the Bar Vendôme. In fact, even before James had arrived at the Académie des Beaux Arts, so he had told me, he had been tipped off that he could top up his bursary by selling his old master copies to a man called Monsieur Armand.

I had smiled when I first heard this from James in Paris; but years later sitting next to an aquamarine swimming pool in California, it was Bud Hardy who had more reason to smile. He explained that of all the people whom he approached at the Louvre, he could probably count on one in twenty leaving Paris with an original copy of their favourite painting. He made it clear that this was because he had been a skilled businessman, an entrepreneur and a man of ideas with a lot of North American know-how. He had even fancied himself as a psychologist. For he claimed to have known instinctively who, among the many foreign visitors to the Louvre, had deep pockets. Indeed, he took pride in assessing who lacked any knowledge of fine arts. And he boasted that he had also been able to sense who might be intimidated, coerced or gently bullied into buying an original copy of a masterpiece in order to suggest that they were cultivated when they were clearly not.

Crucially, Bud insisted that he had never done anything illegal. His clients had returned home with an *original* copy of an oil painting rather than a cheap print. The art students he employed had earned a handsome fee for partaking in an activity that was a necessary part of their study. The only thing that Bud Hardy had been exploiting was a good business opportunity. In fact, Bud reckoned that in the end there was little difference between selling a velvet painting and a copy of a masterpiece. And I had to agree. Both were outside the purview of the art establishment, where expertise, provenance, price tags and aesthetics determined the value of every work. Both were immune from technological analysis. Both were the handiwork of an "anonymous" artist. Indeed, the only difference between these two forms of "art" — so Bud told me — was manifested in how he had then lived.

'Selling velvet paintings had confined me to living in a shabby apartment building on the wrong side of San Diego in Mount Hope — but selling *original* copies kept me in luxury at the Hôtel Ritz in gay Pareee!'

Even so, Bud claimed that he had become bored. It was as simple as that. And that is why he had upped the stakes. This involved a subtle but crucial shift in his procedure. Sure, he had still acquired his paintings in the same way: 'At the beginning of every academic year I made the rounds at the Louvre, singling out the best copyists, like your friend James Conway.' Over the course of the year, Bud would still commission these students to copy specific works. What did change, however, was Armand's clientele.

No longer did he look for them in the Louvre. Rather, acting on the assumption that almost every wealthy person got a frisson from possessing objects that were unique, one-off and with no practical use, he realized that the people who could afford to pay for them were right under his nose.

'I now found my clients in the Hemingway Bar at the Hôtel Ritz.'

Within half an hour of approaching a prospective client, Armand would have dutifully heard their life stories and have ascertained how long his new acquaintances were staying in Paris — and, crucially, whether or not they had visited the Louvre. 'If not,' he chortled at the memory, 'I certainly encouraged them to do so.'

It only took a second chance encounter in the Hemingway Bar for Bud to discover which painting, among the Louvre's vast collection, had been their favourite — oh so often, of course, it was the *Mona Lisa*. If the prospective clients had shown sufficient enthusiasm for this famous painting, backed by sufficient financial means, Armand would invite them to his elegant suite. Then he'd pounce. It would take a couple of evenings, and several bottles of Pol Roger, for Armand to reveal that he had the means of acquiring the *original painting*. And that — for well below the market price — it could be theirs.

As preposterous as Bud's story might have sounded, it seemed convincing when I heard it in retrospect. It had certainly convinced his gullible clients at the time. He would tell them that he had a friend who worked as a night guard at the Louvre; and that friend could exchange a copy of Da Vinci's *Mona Lisa* with the original work, without anyone noticing the difference. It was a clever ruse. 'And it worked more than a dozen times,' Bud claimed, 'because every painting that I sold to my clients was accompanied with a bill of sale officially certifying that their work was *not* an original painting — as they believed it was — but a mere copy. This is how I gave a new meaning to the concept of an *original copy*, Charlie. And everyone was happy!'

How so, I asked? The student copyists continued to enjoy a better standard living. The buyer, he also assured me, had all the excitement of being the only person in the world, besides Armand, to believe that their painting was actually an original. And as for Bud Hardy. He got a hefty commission that allowed him to occupy the Suite Impériale at the Hôtel Ritz. And he had protected himself from prosecution by keeping a duplicate bill of sale verifying that the work was not an original but a mere copy. Ostensibly, therefore, any painting that Bud's wealthy clients had paid well over the odds to possess was nothing more than a copy. It was as simple as that.

Bud Hardy admitted that he had quivered with excitement at the conclusion of every deal. The only catch in his clever scheme would come if any of Bud's clients were foolish enough to show their painting to an expert. And if this had happened it would have taken an art historian only a moment to see that the work was a fake, albeit a pretty good fake at that.

Sure, everyone likes to read about art scandals and art forgeries, when so-called art experts are depicted as pretentious fools and their clients as greedy ill-informed collectors. This would indeed have happened if one of Bud's clients had disclosed that he or she owned the world's most famous painting. If the confession that Bud Hardy belatedly made to me in California had been made public, the consequences would have been predictable. James Conway might have been subjected to a week-long interrogation during which he would doubtless have produced the receipts of the modest fee he received for doing the work.

And what would have happened to the self-styled art expert, Bud Hardy? One could well imagine the worldwide publicity that such a case would arouse. This could have prompted no fewer than fifteen individuals to claim that they owned the *real Mona Lisa*. One might imagine them all in the courtroom — the nouveaux riches couples from Atlanta, Georgia and from Chicago; the up-and-coming businessmen and women from London, from Sydney, Australia and from Argentina; and the Japanese syndicate from Tokyo. And there would be the defendant, Bud Hardy, looking down from the dock at the collection of angry faces and clenched fists of the people who had paid him six-figure sums for a mere copy — multiple copies at that. For in this nightmare scenario, Bud Hardy, alias Monsieur Armand, would surely have been arrested and charged with fraud. I imagined him emerging from the dock, violently waving carbon copies of the bills of sale verifying that every work he had sold had been a copy. Extradited from France to the United States, he might have spent the remainder of his life sleeping on the top bunk in an overcrowded prison.

But, of course, this never happened. Monsieur Armand's clients would never have admitted that their own ignorance had prevented them from realizing that Da Vinci had painted the *Mona Lisa* on wood rather than on canvas. That the artist had used paints that would have been difficult to replicate in the twentieth century. Nor would Monsieur Armand's clients have acknowledged that the bill of sale was all too accurate. Or that while they might have evaded the customs officials in presenting a fake bill of sale when leaving France, they had fallen for a double bluff perpetrated by Monsieur Armand himself.

***

While sitting in a deck chair at the side of the aquamarine pool on the outskirts of San Diego, Bud told me how he had prospered and how he had fooled all of the people all of the time. As in the old days, I found myself hanging on to every word as Bud spun his story in the long session of reminiscence that proved to be my last encounter with this remarkable figure.

81

It was only when I was back in England that the awkward questions formed themselves in my mind — questions that I imagined I would put to him when we met again, for we warmly agreed on a reunion during my next visit to California. And I was already thinking about making Bud Hardy the subject of my third novel. But, not for the first time but definitely for the last, Bud Hardy cheated me out of that expectation. For not more than a month after our seminal encounter, I read of an unusual murder. It wasn't news that a Boston mobster put a bullet through the head of a former art dealer in California. The murder became news around the world because the police had found a crumpled lithograph of the *Mona Lisa* beside the body bearing the following note: "Your murder is an original not a copy".

Nothing is Forever

David had spent the early hours of the morning in the room that he and Beatrice had always called the gallery. He'd now stacked half the couple's art collection against two walls. This was quite enough for one day. David was sweating, his white shirt smelled of yesterday's meetings and he was generally out of sorts for many reasons. But his immediate cause of frustration was because Beatrice was an hour late. He told himself that it was no surprise — just like her, as he should have expected.

Now that it was almost a year since she had left him and made her own life, she no longer conformed to his own standard of punctuality — nor about much else. But David kept his irritation to himself, glad at any rate that they were not quarrelling about the ownership of their joint possessions.

After their break-up, they had agreed that David should become the sole owner of the fine Arts-and-Crafts house that he and Beatrice had shared for more than twelve years. Only a few decades later, any house that overlooked a leafy green square off Hyde Park would fetch several million pounds and be occupied by a Russian oligarch or a Saudi Arabian prince. But in the early 1980s a junior barrister like David had been able to live in the best part of London for a song. He was happy that Beatrice still had the key, happy that she felt free to come and go.

'Sorry I'm late,' he heard her calling out as she let herself in, 'but you know what the Tube's like on a Sunday.' A red-haired woman with a natural loose-limbed composure, Beatrice flung her rust-colored coat into the hall cupboard as though she had just returned from the corner shop with a carton of milk. But she had not been on an errand. Beatrice had spent half the morning travelling to fashionable Mayfair from her nondescript flat in unfashionable Southwark.

David Butterfield, QC, did not care to recollect what it had been like, during his student years, to commute from his equally makeshift one-bedroom flat south of the river to central London on an overcrowded, unreliable and filthy train. He could afford to forget it, now that he enjoyed the privilege of being driven to work. Beatrice had often pointed out that the distance between his home and the Inns of Court could have been covered on foot in half the time that it took David's driver to negotiate London's rush-hour traffic. 'And you might even shed a few of those extra pounds that you're carrying around your waist,' she had told him.

But her husband had clearly got a buzz out of sitting in the back seat of a chauffeur-driven limousine. He was outspoken in refusing to feign sympathy for those less hardworking blokes than himself who had to stand at traffic lights in the rain, or run down the pavement in order to get to a meeting on time.

The eminent lawyer now ignored his estranged wife's reference to the unreliability of London's Underground. He made it clear that they should get down to business by kicking back the third leg of an elaborate display easel on which relevant items from their art collection could be examined.

Beatrice was not surprised when David reached purposefully for one particular painting. The Edward Lear had been their first acquisition. They had bought this landscape painting to celebrate not only their marriage, but also David's admission to the Bar and Beatrice's acceptance as a graduate student at the University of London. Little wonder that, in considering the division of their art collection, they had agreed to look at the Lear painting first.

***

The decision to spend their honeymoon on the island of Corsica had been David's idea. A Napoleon buff ever since visiting Les Invalides in Paris at the age of fourteen, he had wanted to see the birthplace of France's most celebrated military leader. Clutching Felix Markham's recently published biography of Napoleon in his right hand, David had entered the Maison Bonaparte in the island's capital, Ajaccio. Exhibited under the glass-topped display cases were three death-masks and several locks of hair, along with the sort of memorabilia that David had seen in the shops adjacent to the rue Saint-Charles. And that was about it. There was disappointingly little to show that this was where the self-proclaimed Emperor of France had spent the first nine years of his life.

'I felt as though I was walking around a second-hand furniture store,' David had complained to Beatrice as he stuffed Markham's heavy tome into his carry-on. There was nothing in the tawdry museum that he coveted as much as the small bronze bust of Napoleon, purchased on that school trip to Paris and still kept in his pocket as a good luck charm ever since.

'I've got an idea,' Beatrice had suddenly announced to allay her husband's disappointment. It was then that she presented David with a copy of Edward Lear's *Journal of a Landscape Painter in Corsica*, acquired with her customary foresight before they had left London a few days earlier. 'Why don't we follow the walking tour that Lear took around the island on his painting tour of Corsica in 1868?'

And that's how Beatrice and David had spent the next ten days. They had trekked through the Prunelli and Gravona Valleys, they had climbed to the snow line on Monte Cinco and they had followed the mule trail to the Restonica Gorges. At every viewpoint they had attempted to match the scene before them with Lear's line engravings that accompanied his text.

It hadn't been easy. Lear had described the island's mountains as "perfectly clear, gorgeous purple, silver, and blue". But the mountain range that David and Beatrice viewed from the valley floor was shrouded in yellow-brown pollution that had made its way from the Italian coast a hundred kilometers away. The "picturesque" villages, captured so well in Lear's line engravings a hundred years earlier, had become ugly towns dominated by sun-seeking Germans and Scandinavians. Even so, David and Beatrice had enjoyed attempting to see Corsica through Edward Lear's writings and engravings. They had naturally gone on to wonder if they could afford to acquire one of Edward Lear's engravings or, better still, one of his watercolor paintings of Corsica when they returned to England.

In the mid-1980s, if one had a little spare cash, plenty of time and a good eye, a watercolor painting by Britain's most illustrious nineteenth century painter, J.M.W. Turner, could be bought for a few hundred pounds. David and Beatrice not only discovered this. They found that paintings by less distinguished practitioners of British landscape painting could be acquired for even less. Consequently, within a week of returning to Britain, they bought one of Lear's landscape paintings of Corsica in a small gallery off New Bond Street.

If Beatrice and David had wanted to buy an oil painting by Edward Lear, it might have been beyond their means. Luckily, it had never occurred to them to buy anything other than a watercolor. Oil paintings, in their view, were flashy and demanding. They captured the viewer's attention by jumping off the wall. Watercolors, by contrast, were subtle, delicate and evocative. They forced the viewer to go to them. Moreover, as Beatrice pointed out to David, because the artist made no attempt to hide the preparatory pencil sketch that laid the structure for the wash, their paintings had a peculiar charm. 'Yes,' David agreed, 'That's why I like watercolors, they're honest, sort of vulnerable.'

Beatrice and David had been well positioned to enter the collecting game in the early 1980s. They had one good professional salary between them. No costly and time-absorbing children. So that by the time Beatrice had decided to leave David, twelve years after they had acquired their first Edward Lear, the couple had amassed a substantial collection numbering over one hundred watercolors by England's most distinguished landscape painters.

Knowing how to go about collecting them had certainly helped. While other couples did *The Times* crossword at the breakfast table, David and Beatrice studied art auction catalogues, they scanned the newspaper for estate sales and private auctions and they planned their next foray into the remotest parts of England. It was in such out-of-the-way places that they had often convinced the naïve owner of a junk or antique shop that they were more interested in purchasing the frame of a painting than the small masterpiece it surrounded. (They had often giggled all the way back to Mayfair about such coups.) On one of their trips to East Anglia, Beatrice and David had made friends with a wealthy hobbyist art dealer in Norwich. Impressed by the couple's enthusiasm for nineteenth-century English watercolors, Stanhope Cleverly had sought out paintings that matched both the couple's income and their taste.

And it was not just the thrill of adding another picture to their collection that made Beatrice and David quiver with excitement, but finding a place to hang the work when they got home.

'If you leave that painting there, David, it will catch the late afternoon sun and you know that blue is the first color in a watercolor painting to fade.' Another position was eventually found, duly shaded.

'The way you've grouped those pictures makes them look more like a checker-board than a display of fine art,' David complained when he returned home to find that Beatrice had discovered a novel way to exhibit his beloved Turners. The paintings were immediately hung in a single row.

Being well-informed about what they were collecting helped too. Beatrice had grown up surrounded by the work of David Cox, John Sell Cotman, Turner and other masters of the English watercolor tradition. Indeed, this was the reason why she had chosen to pursue a Ph.D. on early nineteenth-century East Anglian landscape painters.

David had no such patrician beginnings. Nor had he any formal training as an art historian. But he had a good eye, he showed plenty of enthusiasm and was now determined to become as knowledgeable as his partner. When Beatrice might occasionally devote her weekend to working on her thesis, David would seek out small picture galleries that might harbor an unknown painting by a major artist.

He had even established a workshop in the box room on the top floor of the house, above the gallery. This was where he had taught himself how to use a fine-toothed saw and miter box; how to measure, then cut, cream-colored mats with a Stanley knife; and how to cover a frame with five coats of gold or silver paint without leaving any trace of the brushstroke. David had not only framed every painting in the collection. He had kept meticulous records of every one of their purchases in a red leather-bound book bought especially for that purpose and lovingly kept up to date through all the intervening years.

***

Indeed, the impressive volume, which had lasted better than their marriage, was now balanced on David's lap. Their agenda for the morning was already clear. They would view and divide half the collection leaving the rest for another occasion. David pointed his pencil toward the Corsican landscape painting by Edward Lear, then looked Beatrice in the eye for the first time since she had arrived.

Elegantly poised on the captain's chair that David had placed several feet from the easel, she was a blur of beige and brown. 'With that bright red head of hair, you'll never be able to wear red or blue,' Beatrice's mother had advised when the young teenager began choosing her own clothes. 'No, dear, it's dusty colors for you.' And that's what Beatrice had stuck to ever since.

'Do we have to decide who gets the Edward Lear now?' Beatrice asked.

'We're not going to get very far if we begin this way,' David muttered to himself as he removed the Lear from the easel, looked meaningfully at his wristwatch, then placed the painting beneath the "undecided" label that he'd attached to the golden oak wainscoting surrounding the gallery.

But after this, things went smoothly. David had once discovered ten John Sell Cotman paintings at an estate sale near King's Lynn in Norfolk. Some depicted herring vessels anchored at the mouth of the River Yale in Great Yarmouth and others the stormy seas off the Norfolk coast. Beatrice judged virtually every maritime picture to be either boring or unsettling. And the works before her, which had been confined to David's upstairs study, fell into that category. Much as David expected,

Beatrice waved her arm before he had finished displaying the Cotmans. He placed all of them under his own label.

As the morning progressed, any work relating directly to Beatrice's long-worked-on Ph.D. thesis was placed under her label. On the other hand, she was happy to let David have the sixteen paintings he had acquired by England's most celebrated landscape painter, J.M.W. Turner. This was because every one of them was either faded or foxed. Moreover, all of them had been executed during the formative years of Turner's career when an accurate transcription of the topography of a scene was foremost in the artist's mind. Thus, there were no bursts of vibrant color; no overlapping of colors to enhance the perspective; none of that delicate rendering of light which had inspired the French Impressionists to do the same thing.

If there had been any of these features, so characteristic of Turner's later paintings, Beatrice might have put her antipathy to the artist's early work aside and claimed half of the paintings for herself. As it was, she cocked her head, causing her ruler-straight hair to cascade over her left shoulder, and said: 'You don't have to put any more Turners on the easel, David, they're all yours now.'

It was just after two o'clock when David helped Beatrice load her share of the booty into a cab. There had been no offer of a drink. No suggestion of having a late lunch at their favorite Italian restaurant just down the road from their leafy square. And there was no farewell hug before the cabbie closed the door.

**

They'd rarely hugged anyway, Beatrice reflected as the cab sped towards the river. A stickler for tradition and the display of good manners, David had never shied away from embracing their friends. It was bear-hugs for the men and sloppy on-the-lips-kisses for any woman who was slow to offer David her cheek rather than her mouth. But when it came to his own wife, Beatrice ruminated as the cab crossed the river and headed south, David's view of connubial sex — 'Couples don't have sex past the age of forty' — had been wounding.

Beatrice had long suspected that her husband's declared antipathy to bodily contact with his own wife, arose from a mild case of Asperger's syndrome rather than frigidity or impotence. And this is why, within a few years of their marriage, Beatrice accepted the fact that she and David had become friends rather than lovers. And this was how she and David had come to expect spending the rest of their lives, directing all of their energies and passions towards collecting pictures until there was no more space on the walls to hang new acquisitions.

Indeed, as the years passed, it was not only the absence of physical contact that became a problem for Beatrice, but where to hang their pictures. David had sought to get around the space problem by hanging the overflow of their collection on the walls of their two guest bathrooms, at least until a visiting art dealer warned: 'If one of your guests takes a shower, the condensation will damage the paintings.'

Later, they had unframed some of the paintings and stored them in coal-black Solander boxes. 'What's the use of buying more pictures if we're going to hide them away in a box?' Beatrice had asked.

Then David had come up with a practical solution. He discarded his fine-toothed saw and miter box, removed all of the wooden frames that he had so carefully constructed in his box-room workshop and replaced them with aluminum frames. 'They're not a patch on the ones you made,' Beatrice observed. But since the sentiment was evidently not shared, she went along with the plan.

Though time-consuming, the adjustable frames did allow David to rotate the pictures between the walls of the house and the confines of the Solander boxes. Initially, Beatrice applauded her husband's efforts and helped him find a new venue for a picture. 'It's as though I'm seeing this picture for the first time,' Beatrice conceded when she noted that David had moved John Constable's preparatory sketch for his famous six-foot long oil painting, *The Hay Wain,* from the Solander box to the top of the staircase leading to the second floor of the house.

However, even this solution proved unsatisfactory. David had recently become a partner in his chambers and his workload had doubled. Meanwhile, Beatrice's academic supervisor had made it clear that she wasn't going to support a further extension for the completion of her student's thesis. This meant that neither Beatrice nor David now had the energy or the time to move the paintings in and out of frames and to take them on and off the walls. Consequently, it was not long before they stopped looking at the artists' work in their collection. Indeed, all that caught their attention were the ugly aluminum frames.

There was one last chance: instead of changing the pictures to fit their home, maybe they could change their home to fit the pictures. Now everyone says that the business of moving house is as disruptive as going through a divorce — indeed that the one may well be an unconscious step towards the other.

Initially, when David suggested buying a house large enough to hang the entire collection, Beatrice was excited. 'Do you think we can now aim for double the amount of hanging space that we have in the gallery?' she asked without expecting a reply, because she sensed that this was what David was now planning to do.

But their enthusiasm for finding a new house proved as short lived as moving the pictures between the Solander boxes and the aluminum frames. As with paintings, so with houses: it became a matter of taste, not easy to resolve. Beatrice wanted a modern house:

'No interfering Arts and Crafts wainscoting, no leaded windows or heavy overhead beams like we've got now. We need white walls and high ceilings. And plenty of light.'

'For God's sake, Beatrice, these pictures were painted in the nineteenth century,' David argued. 'Do you really want to see them displayed on the walls of a white cube?' And then, coming back to her a few days later, David had suddenly relented with a readiness that puzzled Beatrice at the time, but left her uneasy about the whole project. She rejected his offer, unsure of his real motives and perhaps of her own too.

For a while, house-hunting had consumed all of their spare time. It had stopped them from looking at sales catalogues, stopped them from visiting auction houses and private galleries and stopped them from doing anything relating to building their collection. Their London estate agent sensed that the situation was unresolvable before Beatrice and David did. And the agent was proved right, of course, when his prospective clients told him that his services would no longer be required because they were splitting up.

***

It was three months after their first session that the couple met in the gallery to divide the second half of their art collection, including the disputed Lear, of course. Beatrice noticed that David was now wearing a casual light blue shirt. She had often encouraged him to wear blue: 'It will enhance the color of your blue eyes.'

But David had repeatedly replied: 'I'm not in the business of making a fashion statement, Beatrice, and besides, white goes with every tie on my rack.'

She also noticed that he was wearing his hair a bit longer which made his long narrow face look less severe — rather cute, she thought — and she wondered whether he had lost a bit of weight too. Had he given up his driver and limo and begun walking to work? Or was there some other reason for his change of appearance? A quick look around the ground floor of the house on her way to the toilet offered Beatrice no answers. Everything appeared to be just the same. No female hand was evident here.

David had arranged the remaining half of the collection in chronological order. All of it had been acquired during the last six years of their marriage, in random ways. Sometimes prompted by the fact that they'd had a bit more money. Sometimes when a private gallery had approached them, offering a particular painting before it was hung in the show room. Sometimes, flattered by their own skills when attending an art auction, they'd acquired a painting at a knock-down price by knowing when to enter the bidding and when to stop.

And now, after all these random acts of acquisition, there came the equally unforeseen task of dividing what remained of the joint collection. It was a moment that they'd never imagined — all too much like the Roman soldiers who divided Christ's clothing among themselves at the base of the cross. Beatrice and David now found themselves doing the same thing, albeit with nineteenth century English watercolor paintings.

As the morning had progressed, the pictures stacked under David's name steadily outnumbered the works under Beatrice's label. There will be no empty gaps on my walls, David thought as he looked forward to spending the rest of the day hanging a larger share of the collection than he had at first anticipated. This activity, he supposed, might take his mind off seeing Beatrice so beautifully coiffed and immaculately dressed in her dusty colors. It might also be a comfort to him should she refuse to share the shrimp salad that he had prepared just in case she agreed to stay for lunch.

By noon, however, it seemed less likely that Beatrice would take up any such offer of lunch because she seemed to be mentally somewhere else. In fact, it appeared to David that Beatrice had been sleep-walking through the entire viewing.

Beatrice was far from somnolent. She had nodded no more often than yes when David offered a picture for her consideration, if only because the walls of her eight-hundred-square-foot apartment were already crowded with her share of the first half the collection. But this was not the only reason why she did not mind watching David's portion of the collection exceed her own.

During the course of discussing the separation with her lawyer, Beatrice had certainly been advised to claim her rightful share, not only of the house and their joint investments but also of the art collection. 'I'm not a gold digger,' Beatrice had responded.

'You're a single woman now,' the lawyer had reminded her, 'with no immediate prospects of getting a better job…'

'My secretarial job pays the rent,' she interjected, 'and after I've finally completed my thesis, I'll be qualified to apply for a teaching position at a university or college.' Beatrice had cut off further discussion, intoning under her breath, 'It was I who ended the relationship, I who broke the vows, I who must accept the consequences.' She still felt the same, sitting now with the man in the blue shirt, who was dividing the spoils. Likewise, she still felt the pain of losing the man who had been her best friend for so many years. But the fact that he was not even that became clear when David put the remaining painting — indeed the only painting that had been propped beneath the "undecided" label — on the easel.

Beatrice had been unable to take her eyes off it all morning. Created when Edward Lear could turn any bit of mountain or forest scenery into a first-class work of art, this landscape evoked in Beatrice's mind so many pleasant memories. Of Corsica. Of sun-filled days long past. Of their honeymoon when she and David had been so very much in love, so excited about their future.

'No one will ever be able to put us down; from now on we're a team,' Beatrice remembered David telling her during their last day on the island.

'You're my harbor,' Beatrice had whispered later that evening. And, during their flight back to London, she had told him: 'Do you know what, David, within a few years we're going to have the best damn private collection of nineteenth-century English watercolor paintings in the country.'

David now broke Beatrice's reverie, by bringing her attention to the issue at hand. He readily admitted that he had chosen more pictures than she, and that she had readily conceded them to him. 'But I cherish this painting. In fact, I love the Edward Lear more than any other work in the collection.'

'So, do I,' Beatrice responded as she continued to admire the Lear.

What on earth, Beatrice wondered, are we going to do now? She and David sat there, agreed in admiring the delicate wash, the clarity of the light and the contrast between the snowy heights of Monte Cinco and the dark verdant forests covering the valley floor. Were she and David really going to fight over it, like the couple who'd hung on to the legs of a Queen Anne chair until the force of their tug-of-war split it in two?

No, they'd never fought and rarely argued — perhaps, Beatrice sometimes wondered, because there had not been enough passion in their relationship to spark a fight. Should they now simply toss a coin? No,

David hated anything to do with chance. Should they call in someone to arbitrate? David was surely too private for that, always refusing to talk about anything personal to her, let alone to anyone else. Or should she simply let him have the picture to atone for her guilt?

Looking back, Beatrice now saw how much she must have hurt David and for how long. She had been surprised when, after he had learned that his wife was leaving him, David had expressed his grief in uncharacteristically dramatic ways. He had slept in a fetal position on the edge of his side of their bed and cried himself to sleep every night for a week. Then, mustering up all the courage he possessed he had asked, 'Is there anyone else, Beatrice? Is that why you're leaving me?' Beatrice had not replied. She now realized, belatedly, how David had been attempting to win her back by agreeing to move into a modern house. How he had known before she did that their marriage had come to an end and that it was only a matter of time before she announced her departure?

As Beatrice saw it, their separation might well have been easier on David if she had been able to tell him that there was indeed someone else. His friends would have rallied round and invited him to dinner parties where a potential partner would have been served up with the dessert. As it was, David's friends seemed to recoil in bemusement when he told them that the reason that he and Beatrice had split up was, as far as he could tell, because they'd been unable to decide which style of architecture would best suit their pictures.

This seemed little less than bizarre and certainly a feeble excuse to offer them. The situation left an unresolved sense of bafflement among David's friends and colleagues that went beyond the temporary state of social embarrassment that often attends such partings. As a result, David found himself without much-needed support. Even worse — without his best friend, Beatrice, to console him.

***

Although it was now a year since Beatrice had watched — and heard — David express his grief, the intensity of the remorse that she had felt at the time had not diminished. I'll probably be haunted by guilt for the rest of my life, she thought as she and David continued to stare at the Lear. But guilt, Beatrice thought, isn't going to make me give the Lear up.

David broke Beatrice's reverie. 'Why don't we share the painting. You can have the Lear for a year, Beatrice, then—'

'No,' she interjected, 'let's swap the painting every four months.'

David agreed. At last, they had amicably settled the one outstanding issue. David happily escorted Beatrice, clutching the few paintings that she had chosen to take with her, into her cab. He'd now forgotten about the bottle of her favorite white wine that he had chilled, just in case… As for the shrimp salad, the lettuce was no doubt wilted by now.

His thoughts were elsewhere. As he was to have the Lear for the first four months, he could look forward to returning it to the wall facing the bed that he and Beatrice had once shared. Their decision to swap it back and forth like a cherished child might, for a half of each year, deprive him from the pleasure of greeting the painting in the morning and saying goodnight to it before he fell asleep. But it was a rational, lawyerly outcome. And having the painting for half of his remaining life was better than not having it at all.

A week after their second meeting, Beatrice received a list of the pictures that she and David had divided between themselves. It was accompanied by a document setting out the transfer of the Edward Lear picture from one household to the other every four months. Beatrice signed it as readily as she had signed the official divorce papers and returned the document to David immediately.

As agreed, Beatrice had custody of the Lear for the subsequent four-month period. The beloved object found itself no less beloved as a result. Viewing it gave Beatrice so much pleasure that she found herself ignoring the other paintings that hung, three rows deep, on the walls of her apartment. When her four months were up and she had couriered the Lear back to David at her former home, she found herself bereft. She owned three other paintings by Edward Lear but they paled by comparison with his landscape painting of Corsica. 'Why keep the inferior Lear paintings if they give me so little pleasure?' Beatrice asked herself. 'In fact, why keep any of the paintings in the collection when I so rarely look at them?'

It might have proved a passing impulse; but over the course of the next four months, Beatrice resolved to act upon it. She sold some of her collection through Christies and Sotheby's auction houses. She took other pictures back to the gentleman dealer in Norwich. 'My twenty-five per cent commission won't leave you with the sort of money that you and David paid for them,' Stanhope Cleverly told her. Nevertheless, Beatrice parted with thirty paintings.

She gave Constable's sketch of *The Hay Wain* to the Tate Gallery, which owned the oil painting that it had inspired, and she was happy to accept a handsome tax receipt for her donation. Other paintings joined the British Museum's marvelous collection of English watercolors. Although these might be destined to spend the rest of their life in Solander boxes, the museum proved willing to pay Beatrice a reasonable sum to acquire them.

Before it was Beatrice's turn to take possession of the Lear painting for a second time, every painting from her own collection had been sold or donated to public institutions — with only one and a half exceptions. One was the picture that had hung on the wall of her mother's nursing-home suite in Kent. The residual half was her share of the Lear, now hanging opposite David's bed.

While Beatrice had been getting rid of her own collection, David had been making further acquisitions. Having given up looking for a new house, he had spent much of the last year attending auctions, visiting private galleries, renewing contact with gentleman dealers and travelling around the countryside in search of new works. It was on one of his collecting trips in Lincolnshire that David had encountered a hay-laden tractor on a country lane.

North Americans who travel along single-track roads or narrow lanes in the English countryside are often prompted to wonder out loud, 'What will happen if I encounter a vehicle coming in the opposite direction?' There is usually a lay-by, their English friends tell them, where the more courteous of the two drivers can pull over to let the other pass. And if there isn't a lay-by, they continue, the drivers are generally moving at a slow enough pace to prevent a collision.

The narrow lane along which David was driving on that Sunday morning in Lincolnshire had no lay-by. Neither driver was watching the road, nor their speedometers. The ensuing collision punctured the tractor's fuel tank. Sparks flew. The hay on the farm vehicle ignited. The driver pulling the tractor managed to escape. David was not so lucky. His car was awkwardly trapped in an uncontrollable inferno and ended as a burnt-out wreck.

****

David had left everything he owned — his Arts-and-Crafts house, his investments and his collection of paintings — to his former wife. Financially, Beatrice was now unexpectedly relieved of all further worries. But emotionally she was scarred by this grotesque turn of events. Though she had herself ended the marriage, she found herself lonely. She had surprisingly little interest in finding a partner who might fulfill her sexual needs. Moreover, during the last few weeks prior to David's fatal accident, she had begun to hope that they might again become friends.

It took Beatrice some time before she inspected the material possessions that were now hers. Of all the art works, only one painting had a peculiar hold upon her. And that, of course, was the Lear, which at the time of the appalling accident was in David's custody.

It was, therefore, several weeks after the burial, and the subsequent probate of David's will, that Beatrice visited the home that she had shared with her former husband. When she braced herself to enter it, she was immediately surprised to see that the small bust of Napoleon, which David had always carried in his pocket as a good luck charm, was on the mantlepiece. More predictably, the walls of the house were crammed with pictures. David had installed display screens across the gallery, enabling him to hang his entire collection. Why, she wondered, had we never thought of doing this? On closer inspection, Beatrice discovered that, along with David's larger share of their former joint collection, a number of new purchases had been added. These included many of the paintings that she herself had sold to private galleries and collectors or sent to auction.

But one picture that had always hung opposite their bed was missing. The gold hook was on the wall but the Edward Lear painting was not. Beatrice thought that the picture might be "resting" in a Solander box. It was not because David had got rid of the boxes when he had acquired the display screens. Then Beatrice thought of somewhere else that she might find the Lear — at his place of work, of course, in his chambers.

She telephoned one of David's former colleagues, a woman who had run his office and had known his habits. 'It's certainly not here,' she told Beatrice. 'When it was David's turn to have the Edward Lear, he never let the painting out of his sight.' It appeared that David had taken it daily to his office at the Inns of Court; that it had accompanied him to dinner parties, to meetings and to court. 'And there's something else, Beatrice. David even took that painting with him on his weekend jaunts into the countryside.'

Flight

I had hardly imagined that Phyona West would agree to meet a rookie journalist like myself. In those days, she never spoke to the press. She never attended the unveiling of her sculptures, which have given a human dimension to parks and squares, office blocks and government buildings around the world. She was notorious for prohibiting art galleries from displaying preliminary models of her work. And, although Phyona West had been given more than a dozen major retrospective exhibitions, she had snubbed the galleries by refusing to show up on opening night.

Equally unsociable in her private life, the sculptor rarely left her isolated seventeenth century cottage in rural Suffolk. Nor allowed anyone to cross the threshold, with two exceptions. There was Mrs B, who cooked and cleaned for Phyona West five days a week. And there was her immediate neighbour, Colin Fletcher, who was as passionate about publishing books as Phyona was about making art.

The head of Fletcher Publications was what people used to call a confirmed bachelor. Short and squarely built, red cheeked and grey bearded, my favourite uncle is a fuss-budget. And, like his reclusive neighbor, he's a loner.

I've often wondered what I've done to become Uncle Colin's favourite niece. Maybe it's because I read, then report on, all of the books he sends my way. Or because I relish a long and sweaty country walk with him through the hills surrounding his village. Or perhaps Uncle Colin enjoys being congratulated on his superb cooking. 'Another triumph from the kitchen of Uncle Cool' — that's how I've addressed him since the age of four — was no exaggeration. Or maybe I've been an object of envy. At the outset of his career Uncle Colin had joined a major publishing house, starting at the bottom, fresh out of secondary school and spent many years learning the tricks of the trade before setting up his own firm. By contrast, I'm not only the first member of the Fletcher family to have attended university, I have two degrees to my name.

I got the second degree at London's City University. 'Think twice about doing a degree in arts' journalism, Emma,' Uncle Colin had warned me, 'because if you become a journo, you'll spend the rest of your working life chasing stories, then writing them up at break-neck speed in order to meet a press deadline. And what do you think will happen to your beautifully crafted prose once it hits the editor's desk? It will be chopped up and rearranged. And maybe even shredded. Anything too challenging for the paper's average reader will be excised with the stroke of a blue pencil. And if you're lucky enough to get your article published, where do you think it will end up? Not on the shelves of the British Library next to great literary tomes, but in the local chip shop — or in someone's fireplace. This is the best that can happen, but of course, you might not even get a job to begin with.'

It took me five minutes to reject Uncle Colin's advice and then two years to earn my post-graduate degree in arts journalism. Six months after that, I saw my hopes of becoming an arts journalist dashed. My uncle had been right about the difficulty of getting a job in one of the most competitive industries in the country. The only position I was able to land was as a server in an upmarket restaurant in Soho. The job might have been suitable for an actor who was "resting". But I wasn't an unemployed actor. I had no desire to be discovered by a film agent or theatre director while serving up a meal. I was a journalist, or more to the point, an aspiring arts journalist who was desperate to land her first job.

In early autumn Uncle Colin summoned me to Suffolk for a weekend visit. I cancelled a Saturday evening date, for which I'd invested in a new dress and a much-needed haircut. I gave away my tickets for a Sunday afternoon concert at the Albert Hall. And signed off from the Sunday evening shift at Chez Pretentious, as I called the restaurant where I worked.

From the moment I met Uncle Colin at Bury St Edmunds station, it was clear that he had something important to tell me. Was he perhaps terminally ill? Or did his urgent summons have something to do with his business? Maybe Fletcher Publications was in the red. Alternatively, perhaps Uncle Colin was inviting me to join his firm. Yet none of these things seemed plausible. If money was the problem, he could always get a good price for his fashionable London house, smack in the middle of Hampstead. As for my uncle's health, he looked as fit as a fiddle for a man approaching his sixty-fifth birthday. And even if he were ill, he would never have discussed his own mortality. 'It's bad luck to look around too many corners at once, Emma.'

And besides, as we drove from the train station to his village, Uncle Colin was ebullient. He was about to publish the first novel of a woman whose youth and beauty guaranteed that she'd hit the best-seller list and maybe even produce further books with a long shelf-life. He was looking forward to cooking me a good dinner. (When I looked over my shoulder to the back seat of the car, I saw a bottle of Sancerre, a box of Vacherin cheese and the leg of some poor creature, indicating that he'd just visited Harrods' white-tiled Food Hall.) Uncle Colin was also characteristically excited about the route he'd mapped out for our outing later that day. He revealed that it would take us through recently ploughed fields, along a narrow path at the side of a winterbourne and past the edge of a private estate that led to the village pub. 'I trust you've brought your walking boots with you, Emma?'

It was only later, towards the end of our walk, as Uncle Colin was swinging his short legs over the last low-level stile, that he got to the point of his urgent summons.

'I know you've been struggling to make ends meet over the past few months, Emma, and I'd like to help.'

I didn't need reminding of how humiliating it had been to watch most of my university friends land a job with a major newspaper. So, desperate for help, I was all ears. But Uncle Colin refused to tell me how he was going to resolve my employment problem until we'd cleaned the clods of earth from our boots on the boot scraper in front of the Queen's Head pub and were drinking our first pint of bitter. Then he let loose: 'I'd like to commission you to write a biography of Phyona West.'

I was puzzled. I wanted to shout, 'Why me?' Was this Uncle Colin's hard-nosed professional way of making me into a *real* writer, by throwing me into the deep end of the book publishing world? Or was his generous offer fuelled by pity and a sense of obligation to his only sibling, my widowed mother?

There were other things that made me feel uneasy about my uncle's offer. Here was a man who possessed a good nose for what the public wanted to read. Why choose an unknown author when he had a stable of highly experienced and well-known writers to choose from? Why publish a book on an artist whose sell-by-date was about to expire? And why waste time trying to do so when the artist herself would probably be unhelpful to anyone who attempted to write about her life?

Yet apparently Uncle Colin had somehow managed to persuade the country's most reclusive artist to open up her archives, to share her work with and to "tell all" to an unknown writer. Perhaps he had appealed to Phyona West's vanity. Perhaps he had offered her a way to settle old scores. Perhaps he had convinced the ageing artist that it was better to have his own favourite niece, rather than a complete stranger comb through her life — and, if necessary, to hide her dirty linen. Whatever Uncle Colin had done to secure Phyona West's permission, he was now able to offer this tantalising commission to a writer who was a complete novice in the art of biography.

Of course, I knew that Phyona West was not just Uncle Colin's neighbour, but had enjoyed an international reputation. I had often told my uncle about a recurring nightmarish dream that had been prompted after seeing one of her sculptures, years previously, on a school outing to the Tate Gallery.

I couldn't have missed Fiona West's *Flight* when I walked into the gallery because it dominated the glass-domed foyer. Made from one sheet of aluminium that had been bent into a graceful arc, the sculpture's surface was covered with the most vibrant hue of primrose that I'd even seen. Mounted on a six-foot-high plinth that was well above my head, the work appeared to be suspended in space. When I dreamt about it that evening, the sculpture, just like the toys in Tchaikovsky's *Nutcracker Suite*, came alive. *Flight* left its plinth. It circled around the foyer, then ascended so high that it beat its metal wings against the glass-domed ceiling. But the yellow bird, as I would call it hereafter, couldn't escape from its cage. It had split in half, shattered the glass dome, then crashed to the chequered marble floor where I was standing.

***

I met Phyona West the following afternoon. Even before she entered Uncle Colin's low-beamed sitting room I caught a whiff of her *Je Reviens* perfume. And when she swept into the room, wearing a loose-fitting tunic over a full-sleeved peasant blouse that matched the embroidered hem of her skirt, it was obvious that Phyona had dressed to kill. She chose a wing-backed chair in front of the French doors leading to the garden. The absence of direct light on her heavily made-up face knocked ten years off her age. And when she turned towards Uncle Colin, who had taken a brown leather lounge chair next to the fireplace, her profile resembled an eighteenth-century silhouette portrait.

Phyona was strikingly elegant. And she was terrifying. It was difficult for me to imagine how this fragile octogenarian had welded heavy sheets of aluminium together with a propane torch. Or how, as a femme fatale, she had attracted some of the most dashing painters and sculptors of her generation, only to overthrow them each in turn.

Uncle Colin introduced me as 'Your potential biographer,' for I had agreed to write her life story over breakfast that morning.

Phyona shrugged her shoulders, readjusted her posture and laid down her own terms: 'You'll have to watch how you tread, young lady, because many of the people I used to know are still living.' Then she paused for dramatic effect before adding, 'Or half-living.' Phyona West not only put her cards on the table: she explained why so many of them were missing. 'And before you ask me if I have any diaries or journals, I'll tell you right now that I burned them all. But you wouldn't have needed them in any case,' she continued, 'because people are less interested in my life than in my art.'

This wasn't a good beginning and we all knew it. Uncle Colin formed a steeple with his hands, as though offering a supplication to the money god who had always answered his prayers by keeping Fletcher Publications in the black. I wondered if I'd ended my career as a biographer even before I had begun it.

By the time we were drinking tea and eating Uncle Colin's homemade scones, Phyona had agreed to give me access to the work that remained in the barn towering above her thatched-roof cottage. But as she began to talk, it became clear that Phyona West had more to show me than her sculptures. Her reminiscences began to flow like a suddenly uncorked bottle of champagne that had been kept for many years. She even suggested that we move from Uncle Colin's cozy sitting room to the unheated office that formed an appendage to her studio barn. This was no doubt to ensure that I wouldn't interview her for more than an hour. And it worked. It was not only cold in that long-out-of-use office, there was no offer of a mug of tea around which I might wrap my fingers for warmth.

The flow continued on my subsequent visits. Phyona spilled secrets that had long been bottled up. She painted a verbal picture of an era with which I was hitherto unfamiliar. I lapped it all up. Filled numerous spiral notebooks. And when I returned to London at the end of the weekend, I was a little closer to knowing more about the remarkable sculptor.

***

Before she learned to write, Phyona West had turned war-torn London into art. She didn't capture sleeping figures sheltering in the tube stations like the much older artist, Henry Moore. Rather, the young girl sketched the bunker at the back of the garden where she and her family took shelter during the bombing raids. After her evacuation from London at the age of eight to a farm in Devonshire, she captured the high-hedged West Country landscape in delicate watercolour paintings. And when she returned to London just before VE Day, bombsites covered in rusted shards of metal, smashed bricks and rosebay willow-herb became subjects for her art.

Like all artistic prodigies, Phyona needed further training if she were to become an artist. But, after leaving school at the age of sixteen, the closest she got to copying plaster-casts of ancient Greek sculptures, or to sketching from the nude or painting still life assemblages was to appear herself on the modelling platform at the local art school. 'I could hold a pose for an hour without batting an eyelid,' she told me.

With or without her clothes, Phyona West had been much in demand as a model. Within two years she had earned enough money to pay for a month's tour of Italy's major art galleries and Greece's ancient ruins. And after spending two further years modelling for every art college in the city of London, she had saved enough to cover her tuition fees for a year's study at London's Central School of Art. This is where Phyona moved from one side of the studio to the other. 'You can't imagine how good it felt to sit behind the easel and watch the model taking surreptitious glances towards the big railway clock at the back of the studio or attempt to suppress an itch or the need to visit the toilet.'

Phyona's biographical entry in Wikipedia told me that it was only in her second year of study at the Central School of Art that she took up sculpture. 'Why was that?' I asked.

She explained that, when she attempted to sign up for an introductory course in sculpture in her first year, the instructors told her that sculpture was reserved for men: 'It requires great strength, Miss West. And look at you, you can't weigh much more than seven stone.'

'I ignored their warnings,' Phyona told me. 'Strengthened my arms by carrying cement-filled buckets up and down the steep stairs of my family's home.' She had thus convinced one teacher to admit her to his class. Putting aside any false modesty about her admission to the sculpture class, she revealed that, 'During my second year at the Central I showed everyone that I had no difficulty transforming a lump of clay into a perfect likeness of the model. And during my third year, when I was introduced to stone, I wielded a mallet with as much force and skill as my male colleagues,' she claimed. 'Eventually my teachers stopped telling me that sculpture was too physically demanding for a "girl". And that, my dear Emma, is how I trained to become a sculptor.'

After graduating from the Central School of Art, Phyona had taught at a secondary school in the roughest part of London. 'I had to spend most of my time disciplining the students rather than educating them,' she said dismissively. 'At the end of five years I'd had enough of baby-sitting their overactive hormones — so I quit.'

It was after that, as I already knew, that Phyona West had vanished. When I asked her where and with whom she had lived from 1963 to 1965, she gave me that impish smile that I had seen on my first visit, then compared her self-imposed exile to Agatha Christie's disappearance in the 1920s.

'But the famous mystery writer only vanished for eleven days,' I argued, 'while you withdrew yourself from the art scene for two years.'

I made numerous attempts to find out where Phyona had been, and what had happened to allow her to emerge with a new style and a new medium. But all my efforts were in vain.

'If you're wondering why London's Tate Gallery and the Museum of Modern Art in New York bought two pieces of my work when I returned to the art scene in 1965, just look at a few art magazines from the period,' she told me. 'That'll show you what my contemporaries were like compared to me and why I came out on top and they remained at the bottom of the heap.'

Whenever I changed direction and asked Phyona about the men with whom she had lived and worked during her formative years she treated my questions as irrelevant. 'For God's sake, Emma, it was the 1960s. We were in and out of one another's studios — and beds — all the time,' she said with some impatience at my concern for details. 'No one remembered or worried about who they slept with.' Phyona did give me a more direct answer when I asked her if she regretted having never married or having children: 'And give up my art?

Or, worse still, try to do it as a single mother like Barbara Hepworth who had the ill fortune to have triplets and a wayward husband!'

I remember equally vividly her response to my request to have access to any manuscript material that she might not have destroyed. Before she replied, Phyona manoeuvred a thin cigar into a long cigarette holder in order to put as much distance as possible between her lungs and the nicotine, took a long draw, then snapped, 'You've got close enough, Emma! Everyone wants to take a few secrets with them to the grave.'

It became clear after several hours of interviews conducted over several weekends that Phyona was not going to tell me anything more. In some chapters of her life, I would have to rely for facts upon her entry in Wikipedia or on the short articles that announced an exhibition or the unveiling of a sculpture. I was thus forced to build a picture of Phyona West's life from the outside in. So, I studied the Mycenaean sculptures that had enthralled her on that first visit to Greece. I viewed her work in the towns and cities where her own sculptures stood like defiant monuments against traditional and post-modernist work alike. I travelled to St Ives where she had paid homage to an aging Barbara Hepworth and to Perry Green where she'd sought the friendship of an elderly Henry Moore. In short, I talked to everyone who had known Phyona West.

And I got results. Her teacher at the Central School of Art told me: 'She was a natural from the start — ran rings around the other students and eventually around me too.'

Phyona's assistants provided some revealing testimony too. 'We just followed her instructions,' one of them explained. 'This meant doing most of the heavy lifting — and hiding in the barn when her dealer came to visit lest he got the impression that Phyona had not done all of the work herself.' Her assistants bore no grudges. 'None of us complained about this. Phyona paid us well. And when we tired of being her dogsbodies and felt that we had learned enough we all moved on.'

Getting anything out of Phyona's former lovers proved to be more difficult. Some refused to grant me an interview. Those who did agree to see me were reluctant to tell me anything more than when and where their fling with the artist had taken place. But no one I interviewed reported having had any contact, let alone a liaison with Phyona between 1963 and 1965. This left an awkward gap in my account of her life.

At the end of a year and a half, Phyona came to acknowledge me as her chronicler, her biographer — or in less flattering terms for me, as her listening post. Even so, she continued to deny me access to any archival material that might have survived her burnings, as she called them. This left me no closer to knowing what had made Phyona West put her art before her life.

Why she had bought clay rather than food during her student years. Why, as a professional sculptor, she had met time-squeezing deadlines in order to finish a commissioned work while suffering from a raging migraine headache. Why now, in old age, she continued to shun publicity and talked about her sculptures as though someone else had created them. And, above all, why she refused to account for the two years prior to her emergence as one of Britain's most imaginative artists.

It was not enough for me to write that she had been driven by passion; or that, like many successful artists, she was a failure as a human being because at some point she had chosen to put her art above her personal life. Or to fill in the gaps with my own imaginative musings. I owed my uncle more than a run of the mill account of Phyona's life.

***

Even so, the first draft of my manuscript was composed of unverifiable hunches and observations that were strung together with timeworn clichés. During one weekend visit to Suffolk, I expressed my disappointment to Uncle Colin. 'I had hoped to go beyond the hackneyed notion that great art can only come from pain and suffering, depravity and selfishness.'

'But, Emma,' he replied without pausing, 'this is precisely what the public expects to read when they pick up the biography of an artist.'

And when I added that I'd not be able to produce a definitive biography without access to the material that I suspected Phyona had not committed to the flames, Uncle Colin patted me on the back and told me to devote my energies to polishing the first draft of the manuscript.

I returned to London and spent the next month rewriting sentences. I gave more vivid descriptions of the people I had interviewed. I revisited Phyona's sculptures. And I verified everything that she had told me during our interviews. Sometimes this revealed inconsistencies. She had often given me inaccurate dates for her works. She had frequently told me that she had made a particular sculpture on her own when I knew that one of her assistants had done most of it for her. She had also misled me by claiming that she'd spent half a year teaching at the Central School of Art when the school's records revealed that Phyona West had never been on their payroll.

And then there were other lacunae in Phyona's narrative. She refused to admit that, like every other artist before her, she had drawn on other people's ideas. Or that she had shamelessly pitched one private art gallery dealer or potential client against another in order to get better prices for her work. And had stridently insisted that despite receiving many accolades throughout her career, the critics and gallery dealers, along with the general public, had misunderstood her work.

'When it comes to interpreting one of my sculptures,' Phyona opined towards the end of a long interview, 'everyone from the academics, the critics to the general public are a bunch of ignorant fools.'

If I were more charitable, I'd attribute these discrepancies to the unreliable memory of an octogenarian. But Phyona's memory did not appear to be faulty. Why she had misled me —when it was easy to prove her wrong? Why had she played this game with me?

All of this prompted me to wonder how eager I would myself be to "tell all" to my biographer. Would I give access to my teenage diaries which charted my low marks and inability to make close friends during my school years? Would I share the love letters I'd written to an older woman bearing witness to the uncertainty of my sexual identity? Would I reveal that my hopes of becoming an arts journalist were based on the thrill of attending first night concerts, plays and gallery openings — for free. Or, less admirably, on making or breaking someone's career by writing a bad review that caused a theatrical production or an exhibition or a concert series to be cancelled before it had reached the end of its scheduled run? Or would I have the guts to let the world know that I didn't have the cut and thrust to become an arts journalist?

But Uncle Colin didn't give up on me as a biographer. He must have taken seriously my disappointment with what I had written because a month or so later four large binders appeared in the post. Opening them, it became clear to me that he had somehow managed to persuade Phyona to hand over the residue of her archive.

Filed in chronological order were letters of appreciation from well-wishers and former students. There was correspondence from the men, and less frequently from the women, who had helped assemble Phyona's work in the days before she had enough money to send it to a foundry. There were bus and train tickets as well as receipts from an art supply store. There were receipts from her commissions and a boat ticket revealing that she had spent a weekend in Paris during her student years. Had she, I wondered, seen Rodin's *Burghers of Calais* or limited her first visit to the Louvre?

This material helped me to confirm where, when and how Phyona had lived and travelled. I saw that once she could afford it, she always went first class. I now knew how much she had been paid for each of her sculptures — and how little, in turn, she had paid her assistants. But there was nothing that led me any deeper into her private life. Nothing that revealed the source for her ideas that had resulted in the signature works she'd produced in the mid 1960s. Nothing to indicate where and with whom she had lived during those missing years. And nothing to explain why, after becoming such an international success, Phyona West had subsequently become a recluse.

Before I had received the binders from Uncle Colin, Phyona had made it clear to me that our interviews had now come to an end. And to confirm this she had presented me with the working model of that gravity-defying sculpture which had prompted so many of my childhood nightmares. I hoped that giving me the model of *Flight* was a prelude to releasing the rest of her archive and to answering some of the questions that had arisen from my inspection of the documents. But it was a parting gift that signaled the end our relationship. I was thus denied a further interview and we never met again.

***

'I was with her until the end,' Uncle Colin reported two weeks after I had received the four large binders. 'It wasn't particularly sad. She didn't appear to be in any pain. In fact, my dear Emma, just before Phyona died she gave me a cheeky little smile.'

Yes, I knew that smile. It shrouded secrets that had made my life difficult as her biographer. But how, I wanted to ask Uncle Colin, had she looked without her make-up? Just like any other elderly person on their deathbed, would have been his reply. And had Phyona made any sort of confession, I wondered? If she had,

126

Uncle Colin would no doubt have refused to tell me what she had said, for he was a man of the old school.

'I suppose you'll be coming up to Suffolk for the funeral?' Uncle Colin asked me a few days later.

'Of course, I'll be there.'

I had been struggling to find a dramatic ending for the biography. Now Phyona's sudden death and my attendance at her funeral in Lavenham's magnificent wool church offered me several endings. I could focus on the mourners whose voices rose to the wooden hammer-beam ceiling. Or end at the grave side where those who had not already made their way to the Swan Inn for the wake, had gathered for the committal. Or I could recount the eulogies: one given by the director of the Tate Gallery who announced that *Flight* had been returned to the foyer of the gallery; another by Phyona's London dealer who was clearly expecting sales of her sculptures to soar; and, inevitably, a movingly personal one, by my uncle. Rather to my own embarrassment, but no doubt in a professional move to ward off other potential authors, Uncle Colin had announced that his niece was about to publish a "definitive" biography of Phyona West.

I was making a mental note of these various ways to frame my ending when, walking towards the Swan Hotel, I was approached by a man and a woman. I had seen them sitting in the back row of the nave during the service. Then, after the committal, I noticed that they had been among the last to leave Phyona's grave. They weren't local villagers, nor gate crashers hoping for a free glass of bubbly at the wake. Rather, there was something about the way they were dressed — the man's broad-rimmed fedora and checked scarf, his younger companion's down-to-the-ankle cotton skirt — which suggested that they might be paying farewell to a fellow artist.

'Your uncle indicated that you're Phyona's biographer,' the small-statured, leather-faced man said to me in what I recognised as a sing-song West Country accent. 'Now that she's dead you might like to hear about some of the things that could not be said while she was alive.'

I hoped that they didn't hear me sigh. At an earlier stage such an offer of help would have been welcome; but at this point the book was all but finished and, once I had written the epilogue, it would be signed off at the press. The publication date was set. Uncle Colin had already booked a room for the launch at the Ritz. I'd bought a dress that avoided presenting myself as a thirty-year-old black-stocking. Pre-publication posters had been plastered around London — I'd had to hold myself back from shouting 'I wrote that book' when I passed by multiple images of the cover while descending the escalator in King's Cross tube station. Besides, I was already looking forward to writing someone else's life story, providing, of course, there were plenty of manuscripts and, above all, that my subject was dead.

Even so, it had not been easy leaving Phyona's world. I missed my purposeful visits to Suffolk. I even missed negotiating my way around an interview in hopes of getting Phyona to tell me something new. Ever since her death, I had attempted to bring her back to life in my dreams. But it was hardly satisfactory because as she was always about to tell me what had happened during those missing years, I suddenly found myself wide awake. Even at this late stage, then, if these two strangers had more information, I knew that I had to listen.

'I'm Geoffrey Cameron,' the man had said, 'and this is my daughter, Sarah. You will never have heard of me — though back in the 1960s I was one of the first artists, along with Anthony Caro, to make sculptures out of Cor-Ten steel.'

Turning away from the large and fashionable Swan Inn, now buzzing with the chatter of Phyona's admirers, I suggested that we three climb the hill to the Angel Pub which dominated the Market Square. Fortunately, the locals had not yet arrived for their daily pint and game of dominoes. We sank into three comfortable armchairs in front of an open fire and stretched out our hands for warmth.

'Yes, Tony Caro remained in London and became famous while I moved back to my childhood village in Devon and vanished from the art scene. That's not to say that I stopped making sculptures and even selling a few,' Geoffrey continued, 'as Sarah here can testify.'

The woman, whom I reckoned to be in her mid-forties, blushed, then nodded in agreement.

So why were they telling me all of this? Were the Camerons trying to cash in on Phyona's fame by getting me to give them a walk-on part in my book? Was Geoffrey a disgruntled lover seeking revenge? Or was there something else they wanted to tell me?

'Phyona gave up teaching a few months after we met at a party in Soho,' Geoffrey continued, 'and that's when she decided to move down to Devon with me in 1963.'

I was suddenly fully focussed on Geoffrey's story. This was clearly an important relationship, of which I had been totally unaware. But I didn't realize how important it was until, a few seconds later, Geoffrey took three heavily-creased photographs from his breast pocket. The first showed a scrappy bit of unmoved lawn on which was displayed a Cor-ten steel sculpture. The second photograph, taken a year later, featured one of Phyona's brilliantly colored u-shaped aluminium sculptures.

Was Geoffrey now claiming this as his own creation?

Before I had a chance to ask, Geoffrey pointed to the second photograph and made it clear that this was no simple charge of plagiarism. 'I tried to persuade Phyona to stick to Cor-ten steel,' and to reinforce the point that she was more accomplished in that medium than himself, Geoffrey pointed to the first photograph.

'But she didn't like the way Cor-ten steel turned rust-brown when it was exposed to the elements. Phyona wanted colour,' Geoffrey continued as he produced a third photograph. 'As she always said, the brighter the better. She also wanted a more malleable material and that's when she started working in aluminium.'

The photographs were in fairly good condition and I was already planning where they could be integrated into my book when Geoffrey indicated that there was something more that he wanted to tell me.

'It did not take me long to realise that Phyona had broken new ground and I even began working in aluminium myself. But my sculptures were little more than copycat versions of hers. Of course,' Geoffrey continued, 'Phyona feared that if we exhibited our work together, she'd be dismissed as my muse. She told me that she'd worked too hard to become another Camille Claudel, whose own sculptures inspired her lover, Rodin. And this is why she left two-year-old Sarah and me. Why she moved back to London where she soon rocked the art world with her vibrantly painted sculptures.'

It was at this point that Geoffrey handed me a fourth photograph. It featured a young woman standing next to a wicker bassinette. Sarah blushed for the second time within ten minutes, when her father presented me with a copy of her birth certificate.

Phyona West's commitment to her art had clearly eclipsed her commitment to her family. I was shaken.

This was not quite the story I had expected to hear when I agreed to talk to Geoffrey Cameron and his daughter. And it was certainly not the story that I had told in my book.

***

Geoffrey lent me the photographs along with a copy of Sarah's birth certificate. He also agreed to meet me in London the following week. I now had a sinking feeling that I'd be making a call to my editor the following day. But altering the manuscript at this late stage would push back the publication date; it would make a mockery of my uncle's well-publicised autumn publication list. Yet if I did nothing and the truth emerged after the publication of my book, would anyone have confidence in my skills as a researcher when I'd made such an omission?

And yet, pushing such misgivings aside, I found myself elated when I returned to Uncle Colin's cottage following the wake. I now had the answer to my unresolved dream. Between 1963 and 1965 Phyona West had given birth to a daughter. She'd turned from working in Cor-ten steel to aluminium. And she'd not been a muse to Geoffrey Cameron but the mother of his daughter.

If I expected my uncle to be as thrilled as I was about this new information, I was wrong. 'You can't change things at this late stage, Emma,' Uncle Colin barked. 'And besides,' he added in an attempt to sweep the matter under the carpet, 'Phyona would turn in her grave if we published what you've just told me.' But Uncle Colin's real concern was hard-headed rather than soft-hearted. 'Just think of how people would feel about owning a work created by someone who'd abandoned her daughter for the sake of her art!' he demanded. 'And what would it do to future sales of her work — not to mention the reception of your own book?'

I said at once that I could not walk away from Geoffrey and Sarah Cameron. 'After all, we don't even know whether or not Phyona had any further contact with Geoffrey or her daughter,' I responded. 'Their lack of bitterness, their willingness to meet me again shows that they are not simply pursuing a grudge — and anyway, I've already arranged another interview with them next week.'

'But how many interviews will there be after that? And how many months will it take you to revise the manuscript? No, Emma, that's simply not possible.'

Riding the train back to London later that day, I couldn't get Sarah Cameron's soft brown eyes and her dignified demeanour out of my mind. What was I going to tell Sarah and her father now? That I could not integrate their story into my book because the prissy head of Fletcher Publications, my very own much-loved uncle, preferred a cover-up? Or should I save my own face by claiming that my book could not be altered because it was already at the press? Or, more candidly, that Sarah and Geoffrey should go back to the obscurity from which they had momentarily emerged because the world wasn't ready to accept the fact that Britain's leading female sculptor had abandoned her family for the sake of her art? Or, more truthfully, that if Phyona West had been a male artist, the public would have no difficulty accepting the abandonment of her lover and daughter.

Everyone knows the outcome, because my biography was indeed published without any revision and became a bestseller. It not only enshrined the Phyona West mystery about her disappearance and confirmed her posthumous status: it made my reputation as the kind of biographer who could be trusted to tell all. For among the glowing reviews, the one that Fletcher Publications chose to put on the cover of all the reprinted editions of my book simply says: "At last, here's a book that gives us the *real* story of Phyona West's life". Uncle Colin, a good neighbour to the end, was so pleased.

Against the Grain

Sam knew all along that he would have some trouble in gaining parental approval for what he was up to. He had duly completed his course at art school by the time he made his first black box, and was now working for a year in a ramshackle studio generously made available by his father. A perfect cube, the box would have looked good standing next to a reclining Breuer chair or an Ercol daybed. But Sam's cube wasn't a side table, still less a coffee table or a footstool. It was a work of art.

'Is that all you've got to show me after nearly twelve months?' Rex Smith demanded on a rare visit to his son's studio as he rubbed a sawdust-covered shoe against the back of his perfectly creased trouser leg. Then he thought again. Sam was his only child. Charlotte had given her life for the boy. He wasn't bad, just different. Rex lowered his voice, now adopting a more conciliatory tone to soften his uncharitable remark: 'So what does the box represent, son?'

Sam could see that his father was uncomfortable standing amidst the carpentry shavings, the cans of wood stain and scraps of sandpaper. He wasn't going to make things worse by giving him a lecture on how the box represented absolutely nothing. That its meaning was that it had no meaning. That the box could not be reduced to a workmanlike subject or theme. And that, like other examples of Minimalist art, the box was all about doing, about making, about travelling to — rather than arriving at — a destination. Nevertheless, Sam needed to secure a further year's funding from his father so, he took another tack, one that a man who had cornered the market in the pencil industry might understand.

'You know a thing or two about wood,' Sam began. 'Now this box is made out of Brazilian ironwood.'

'Never heard of it, son', was the unpromising reply from the tall, broad-shouldered, fair-haired man who prided himself on standing no nonsense in his trade.

'Well, it's one of the most difficult woods to work with,' Sam continued briskly, seizing the initiative for once. 'For a start, it's as tough as nails.'

And to prove his point Sam picked up a discarded piece of ironwood from the studio floor, stubbed out his cigarette on its smooth surface, then blew away the ash. Rex was duly impressed by what he saw. The cigarette had left no trace whatsoever on the wood.

'Ironwood's also heavy, Dad.'

Sam chucked the same piece of wood into a bucket of water. It sank immediately. So far, so good.

'And if you spend enough time sanding Brazilian ironwood and polishing it like this,' Sam enthused as he pointed to his box, 'you get a satin-smooth finish!'

Rex ran his finger over the box's lid. Yes, it was as smooth as a kid glove. And as he continued to rub his finger back and forth across the orangey-brown coloured wood it became as warm as the electric blanket that kept his feet cozy during the cold winter nights. Perhaps there was some hidden use to which this exotic wood might be put?

'But, for me personally,' Sam continued, 'the most amazing thing about Brazilian ironwood is that it can be transformed into any colour that I want. Of course, it's a slow process, Dad. Every coat of stain that I apply takes more than a week to dry.'

After Sam had made his case, his father took a deep breath. He needed time to decide whether this marijuana-smoking young man was worth supporting for another twelve months. More immediately, and more surprisingly for a man who had spent years making weekly visits to the floor of his pencil-producing factory, Rex needed fresh air. Ironwood was something new to him. Its peculiar scent, when mixed with turpentine, paint stain, wood dust — and also with pot — had made him feel dizzy. He walked towards a half-opened window at the back of the studio and looked out. In the distance, rising above the forests that fed British Columbia's timber industry, were the North Shore Mountains. In front of this Wagnerian back-drop was the façade of the glass-fronted office tower that Rex had built in the centre of town. And directly below

Sam's studio were a series of shallow-roofed warehouses and factories.

Rex Smith had begun his apprenticeship as a pencil-maker in one of those buildings. It was where he'd made his name — and his fortune — by inventing a machine which wrapped thin slats of cedar around fragile graphite rods. 'Never thought my only child would begin his career on the east side of the city, too,' the fair-haired man mused. He turned around and took another look at the shabby furniture, the propane burner and the chipped porcelain sink. Then he looked at his son. Sam's small delicate frame, high forehead and long dark hair reminded him of his long-deceased wife.

'I'll give you one more year, Sam.'

And after that? Sam wondered. It was better not to ask.

***

As it turned out, Sam had not needed to appeal to his father for further support. When he got a spot in the student exhibition at The Aries Gallery, his wooden cube was the only work that sold. And the story was that it sold for far more than was expected because more than one of Mr Cunningham's clients had wanted it.

Admittedly, the gallery's owner and director hadn't anticipated selling anything. His annual *Up and Coming* Exhibition, featuring the art students' graduation pieces, was mounted as a goodwill gesture, not as a money-maker. The critics usually ignored it. The gallery's blue-chip clients rarely ventured into the back room where the *Up and Coming* exhibition was confined like an aberrant child to the back of the classroom.

But Charles Cunningham was nothing if not pragmatic. 'Got any more cubes?' the short-statured, open-faced, business-suited gallery dealer asked Sam after the week-long exhibition closed.

'No,' was the artist's baffled reply, 'this is the only one I've made.'

Cunningham was impatient of such unworldliness. 'Well, get busy and make a few more — I've got three clients who've each signed up for one of your boxes.'

Sam knew that every artist in town wanted to be taken on by The Aries Gallery. He also knew that Mr Cunningham got his stable of artists the highest prices for their work in town and gave them plenty of publicity in the local papers and national art magazines. Even so, Sam was reluctant to begin his career producing works of art by the dozen, like a farmyard hen laying a crateful of eggs. He might well be proud of his half-by-half-by-half-metre cube, polished as smooth as a river stone, then painstakingly painted with fifteen layers of furniture stain. But did he really want to manufacture another, then another, then another box? And, as for money, it wasn't a problem now that he'd sold his first black cube and had elicited a year's support from his father.

Sam only stepped down from his moral high ground when Charles Cunningham convinced the country's leading art journal to feature the Minimalist work on the cover of its magazine.

'I'll produce another box for your gallery, Mr Cunningham. But in my own time, at my own pace.'

The director happily fostered the belief that he was taking a big chance with this scraggly-haired strong-minded young man. But Cunningham was no fool. The artist's proclaimed indifference to money, to fame, along with his unwillingness to meet his fawning admirers, fitted the identikit of the temperamental artist. The shrewd gallery dealer now made the most of Sam's reclusive lifestyle, eked out on the upper floor of a disused warehouse. He boasted about the skill that it took to match every grain of wood at the corners of the box and readily exaggerated how long it took Sam to sand, then glue, then stain every thirty-centimeter-wide plank of Brazilian ironwood. He also hinted, without revealing, how a secret combination of wood stain and oil gave Sam's box its satin finish. And when Sam refused to be interviewed by the press or to meet with a potential collector, Mr Cunningham's clients were readily persuaded that this added to the artist's mystique — and to the monetary value of the young man's work.

Sam's second box duly went on display at The Aries Gallery twelve months after the first. There was so much interest from prospective purchasers that the gallery director, with convincing reluctance, explained that he was forced to hold an auction. The unwitting collectors duly played their part in his scenario by bidding against one another so aggressively that they tripled the original asking price. Those who were unsuccessful had to wait another year for one of Sam Smith's black cubes to be put on the auction block. They also had to be prepared to dip deeper into their pockets as the price for a box by Sam Smith seemed set to rise year by year.

Sam was in his element. He appeased Mr Cunningham. He worked at his own pace and in isolation. And, best of all, he did not have to think about altering his style in order to keep up with the latest trends. Thus, Neo-conceptualism, Neo-expression, Post-modernism, Land Art and every other new movement passed Sam by. The politically correct art police and the censors were never on his doorstep. After all, what could anyone find offensive about a black cube? And Mr Cunningham's clients, who seemed as unwilling to embrace new styles and new modes of expression as the artist himself, were each happy to possess a piece of art that proclaimed a timeless appeal.

As the years raced towards the end of the twentieth century, Sam showed himself tireless in producing one well-made box after the another. Patience made for perfection in a process that developed its own mystique and brought its own satisfaction. The aroma of the Brazilian ironwood was as intoxicating as success itself. The glue used to join the pieces of wood gave Sam a pleasant high. The artist's exposure to the wood's pungent oil gave his dark hair a fashionable yellow hue. The act of pulling and pushing a piece of sandpaper over the rough surface of the wood might seem a simple task; but hearing the swish, swish, swish and the rasp, rasp, rasp that accompanied every movement was mesmerizing. Above all, watching the smooth surface of orange-tinted wood take on, with each coat of stain, an ever-deeper hue of brown — some called Sam's boxes black — became a thrilling exercise in revelation of a box's immanent identity.

Then there were the incremental changes that made any sense of boredom quite inappropriate. Sam began using a finer grade of sandpaper. He began polishing the wood with an electric machine. He altered the texture of his boxes by adding a little wood dust to the varnish. And, more radically, Sam started to increase the size of his cube by half a centimetre every year.

'I know what you're doing, Sam,' Mr Cunningham told the artist on one of Sam's rare visits to the pristine, white-walled gallery. 'You may be bored making the same thing again and again, but remember I've got clients out there who've been waiting years for one of your boxes. They don't want change; they expect the one that I sell them to be the same size as the boxes owned by their rival collectors. In any case, if you start making your boxes too large, they won't fit into people's living rooms.'

The artist seemed unimpressed. He knew that anyone who could afford to pay a six-figure sum for one of his works had more than enough space to accommodate a larger box.

'And don't think that I'm going to pay you more just because you're your boxes are a bit bigger,' was Mr Cunningham's parting shot.

Sam ignored such warnings. He continued to experiment with new stains and varnishes. He continued to polish his boxes with an electric sander. And he continued to increase the size of his cubes. Sam did these things because he knew that, despite Mr Cunningham's protestations, the gallery owner had a reputation for treating paintings and sculptures like pieces of carpet — the larger the work the higher the asking price.

Initially, Sam's modifications were so minor that no one but Mr Cunningham noticed. Eventually, however, everyone caught on to what Sam Smith was doing, which itself renewed interest in his work. Before the unveiling of a new box the art critics would ask: 'How many layers of stain has he use this time? Is Sam still using Brazilian ironwood or is he using another kind of wood?' Above all, they would ask: 'How many centimetres has Sam increased the size of his box this year?'

For his millennial piece, Sam not only made his box larger, he abandoned the cube altogether and produced a two-by-one-meter rectangular box. This further shift

— or, as some preferred to call it, evolution — prompted the curators and board members of the city's leading public art gallery to take a new interest in Sam Smith's work. They approached Mr Cunningham with the idea of acquiring the rectangular box for their permanent collection. A delighted Mr Cunningham asked his regular clients, as a public-spirited gesture, to allow the gallery to jump ahead of the queue. They agreed to do so. After all, the public gallery's acquisition assured them that they would be making a good investment when they eventually acquired a work by the reclusive artist.

The exhibition of Sam's rectangular box was a landmark event. The art critics loved it and gave Sam plenty of copy in their newspapers and magazines. The public, who formed a snake around the block-wide public gallery, loved it. The gallery's board of directors were thrilled when the number of visitors reached an all-time high. And Sam Smith's father was over the moon.

No one attended the exhibition more frequently than Rex Smith. Now semi-retired, he popped into the gallery twice a day. He urged — some would say bullied — his non-art-loving colleagues who worked in the pencil-making warehouse and in the shiny office tower to see his Son's show. And, on one of his rare visits to Sam's studio, he asked his son to make him a box.

'You know that I'm under contract with The Aries Gallery, Dad.'

'But can't you do one for me, on the side, in your spare time, Sam?'

'How can I do that when I'm working my ass off to produce one box a year?'

Year by year, following Sam's exhibition at the public gallery, Rex Smith repeated his request. And year by year Sam disappointed the person who had given him a set of blocks when he was a toddler. Who had allowed the boy to play with his much-coveted carpentry tools? Who had paid his son's way through art school, then supported him during those two crucial years, following his graduation? Who had come to accept the fact that his only child would probably spend the rest of his life holed up in a semi-derelict warehouse surrounded by shabby furniture, a two-ring propane burner, and a chipped enamel sink? Who would continue to eat most of his meals in the diner down the street? Would seldom bother to telephone him. And who would live in such isolation that as far as Rex Smith could tell, Sam's only friends could be counted on three fingers.

***

Sam's friends were a mixed bunch. None of them had the privilege of being full-time artists. Following art school, Charles Brown had studied interior design and was now running one of the best furniture stores in town. 'I sell cubes too,' he liked to remind Sam. 'They're made out of plastic or laminated wood and cost a fraction of what Cunningham charges for one of your boxes. And however much my clients like to think they are buying a well-crafted piece of furniture, most of the stuff in my showroom was made on an assembly-line in Malaysia.'

The second former classmate, who had maintained a link with his reclusive friend, was applying his artistic skills to the high end of commercial design. After leaving school Bertie Jennings had set himself up as a web designer. In a few years, he was earning more than all of his former classmates put together.

'I may be rich,' he told Sam. 'But I'm not famous. And I'm anything but free.'

Bertie had initially enjoyed visiting his clients' offices and factories, reading the minds of a firm's board members, then coming up with a logo. But, over time, the fact that his name rarely appeared next to any of his award-winning designs began to grate. The boy who had come out of art school at the top of the class may have acquired a small fortune, but he was no longer the most promising art student because he wasn't an artist at all. Bertie Jennings had become a slave to art-blind, aesthetically numb boards of directors whose only goal was to increase the company's profits.

Like many of Sam's former classmates, Tom Carr went on to teach art. 'Sam Smith and I were students together,' the stocky full-bearded teacher boasted when Minimalist art was the subject of his lecture. And if his students pronounced Sam Smith's work boring and repetitive, Tom came to his friend's defence.

'Sam Smith knew before the rest of us that Art, with a capital A, had come to a dead end. That the notion of development, change and uniqueness was better suited to work produced before the sixties. That any attempt to capture the uniqueness of a country like Canada was best left to the Sunday painters and their more successful predecessors, the Ontario-based Group of Seven and their followers. And that what we've ended up with in the twenty-first century is a genetically-modified art. It's easy to create. It's easy on the eyes. And it's tasteless.'

This is how Tom Carr justified his friend's tireless production of the cube, and more recently of the rectangle, to his students. Most of them agreed that art had come to an end until they went back to their studios. That's when the urge to create something new, to give the world a new vision kicked in and they began re-inventing the wheel.

Once a month Charles, Bertie and Tom took the rickety elevator to the top floor of Sam's warehouse studio. It was a welcome break from their partners, from their young children and from the uneventful routine surrounding their lives. After making themselves comfortable on Sam's couch, or in one of his over-stuffed threadbare chairs, they drank a bottle or two of red wine and shared a joint. Since Sam was the only one among them who regularly smoked pot, he knew where to get the best weed in town.

They talked well into the night recalling the peculiarities of their former teachers and classmates. And, in an effort to convince Sam that they were still practising artists, Charles, Bertie and Tom talked about the paintings and sculptures that they were creating in their spare time. None of them brought their work to the monthly meetings at Sam's studio. None of them admitted that their work was only shown at the local community hall, in the church basement or in the window of a picture frame shop alongside the paintings and sculptures of amateur artists like themselves. No wonder the silent thought arose that their successful friend might perhaps put in a word for them at The Aries Gallery.

It was Bertie who went beyond hoping when, after consuming more than his share of the wine during one visit, he suggested that his old friend ask Mr Cunningham to give them a group exhibition. 'In fact,' Bertie continued, 'I've even got a catchy title for our show. It could be called *Four Old Time's Sake*.'

Bertie's suggestion that he exhibit alongside his former classmates at what Sam considered to be *his* gallery fell on deaf ears. He responded by stubbing out his joint on the floor with the heel of his boot. Then he stood up, rubbed the palms of his hands against the sides of his baggy jeans and looked towards his unfinished box. Sam's thought was all too obvious. If these guys would only leave, I'd have time to put another coat of stain on my box before going to bed.

Sam's gesture signaled that the evening had come to an end. Five minutes later Charles, Bertie and Tom were riding shoulder to shoulder down to the ground floor of the warehouse in the cramped elevator. Ten minutes after that, they were huddled around three sleeves of beer in a nearby pub.

'There's nothing to prevent us from holding an exhibition on our own,' Bertie suggested defiantly as he pulled the loops on the terry-toweled tablecloth. 'In fact, I've got a brilliant idea for our first show. And I've even thought of a name for our group: we could call ourselves The Collective Eye.'

Within a couple of weeks, the three men had rented space — at Bertie's expense — in one of those fly-by-night, off-gallery-row venues that cater to experimental art and to artists who can't get an exhibition at a proper gallery. It was here that Bertie, Tom and Charles mounted their first exhibition. Rather than each showing individual pieces of their own work, they had joined forces.

The Collective Eye's installation had a haunting sense of familiarity. It consisted of two over-stuffed chairs and a sagging couch. There was a chipped porcelain sink and a one-ring propane burner. The wooden floor was strewn with power-saws and electric polishers, wood shavings and bits of sandpaper along with cans of furniture stain and oil. And illuminating the installation from the back wall was a ray of light from a half-opened window. The exhibition's title was simply, *Studio Garret*.

Whose garret? — that was the tease. Most art lovers were familiar with Van Gogh's vibrant blue and yellow bedroom-studio in Arles, which the artist had turned into art more than once. But neither reporters, art critics, officials at the public art gallery nor Sam's own dealer, Mr Cunningham, had ever seen the place where the town's most famous artist ate, slept and created his work. Now, with the *Studio Garret* on show, the veil was lifted. No one was left in any doubt as to whose studio had been recreated, if only because smack in the centre of the installation was a black rectangular box.

Photographs of The Collective Eye's installation appeared in the national press and in glossy art magazines. People who had never entered a gallery in their life lined up to see the show. Charles, Bertie and Tom rented the exhibition space for another month so that everyone could see their installation. And the city's public art gallery, which had acquired Sam's first rectangle box a few years earlier, added *Studio Garret* to their permanent collection and immediately put it on show.

One might have thought that the attention given to The Collective Eye's installation would have prompted more interest in Sam Smith's boxes. But the opposite happened; the spell had been broken. Perhaps it was because the process by which Sam made his boxes was no longer a mystery. The names of the stains, the oils and the varnishes were now there for everyone to see. So were his power tools and various grades of sandpaper. Comments written in the guest book at the entrance of the exhibition were all too explicit: 'I could do that' and 'Hell, anyone can create a black box if they have access to the right tools!'

Only a few critics came to Sam's defence. They cried appropriation and betrayal. They condemned the public gallery for removing the faux black box which Tom Carr had made for the installation, and replacing it with the authentic Sam Smith box the gallery had acquired a few years earlier.

Things were made even worse for Sam when his most loyal supporter, Charles Cunningham, sold The Aries Gallery. During the process of rebranding the business and making a name for herself during the process, the new owner put the gallery's old cash cows — among whom was Sam Smith — out to pasture.

True, some less prestigious art galleries invited Sam to join their list of artists. But he declined. He'd made all the money that he'd need for the rest of his life. Anyway, he reckoned, when the proceeds from the sale of his art ran out, there was a hefty inheritance coming to him from his father's estate. Besides, Sam not only welcomed his freedom from a years-long commitment to The Aries Gallery: Sam wanted to do something else.

'This one's for you,' his eighty-five-year-old father was told during his next — and last — visit to his son's studio.

The box that Sam had just finished was enormous. It had required more trips to the lumberyard and more cans of paint stain and varnish. There had been eyebrow-raising gestures from the concierge, who had recently been installed in the warehouse after developers had convinced their rich apartment-seeking clients that it would be cool to live cheek by jowl with the renowned artist who occupied the top floor of the building. Grudgingly, the concierge had removed the top of the elevator cabin so that Sam could squeeze his planks of Brazilian ironwood into the confined space; the pots of glue and stain, that now filled the lift, were tolerated. The tenants who were forced to walk, rather than ride up to their apartments, were told that the elevator was occupied by the mad artist on the top floor.

Memory and meaning had never been part of Sam Smith's work. It had always been the doing, the process, the making itself, which mattered. So, as the wood for his father's box became smoother, following multiple sandings, the artist was reminded of how, on that first visit to his studio, his father had rubbed his hand over the wood and felt its warmth. When Sam swept the shavings from the floor, he remembered how irritated his father had been when he'd seen the fine dust of the ironwood covering his shiny black shoes. When Sam became aware of the intensity with which he was working on Rex Smith's box, he remembered how his father had never called him to dinner, or reminded him that he had homework to do, or ordered him to clean up his room when he was sawing, sanding or polishing a piece of wood in the garage workshop. And when Rex Smith died a day after his large rectangular box was finished, Sam thought how ironic it was that his father would himself end up in a kind of box.

Sam had often wished that his clients could see that he gave as much attention to the interiors of his boxes as to the exteriors. To prove his point, he climbed inside the box. It was, he thought, a pity that Rex Smith would not be able to enjoy his son's largest work to date. It was left for Sam to feel its smooth sides, as smoothly sanded as the exterior; and left for Sam to get a whiff of the sweet spicy scent of the Brazilian ironwood mixed with the oil of the stain. It was left for Sam to note that, unlike the box's exterior, the colour of the interior would never turn a darker hue. Finally, when Sam slid the lid into place above his head it was left for him to appreciate, how it formed an air-tight seal, how it fitted so snugly that, once it snapped into place, even the maker himself would never be able to escape from his own tomb.

Why Not?

It all began while I was being fitted for my first suit. I was excited about exchanging my scratchy knee-length breeches for down-to-the-ankle-trousers. For even in material-strapped post-war Germany no one beyond the age of fifteen wore *kurze Hosen*. I was excited for another reason too. I was about to enter employment in the most prestigious private art gallery in West Berlin.

It's not as though I had any other choice. No one like me, born into the Wenshoffer family, had the luxury of doing anything else, especially not if they happened to be the only child of Hilda and Anton Wenshoffer themselves. So, I put aside my wish to become a mathematician and, as soon as it was legally possible to do so, I left my studies, my friends and my carefree life at the gymnasium and kept the appointment that had been made for me at Koch and Sons tailors.

My grandfather had established the first art gallery devoted to nineteenth-century German painting just before the unification of Germany in 1871. Ever since then, the Wenshoffer Gallery had been selling paintings that wallowed in the nationalist sentiment of the day: Bavarian peasants wearing broad-brimmed hats; parlour maids listening for a bit of gossip at an open door; light-filled mountain landscapes with a stag or two; and families enjoying a day's outing to the North Sea.

Grandfather Wenshoffer and his son, Anton, had made a handsome profit selling these benign pictures to people in the upper echelons of German society. And things got even better for the Wenshoffers in 1933. That's when Adolf Hitler became Chancellor of the Third Reich. During the next few years "undesirables", as the Nazis called them, who were forced to leave town carrying nothing larger than a suitcase, sold their paintings to the Wenshoffer Gallery for well below the market value.

If the Wenshoffer Gallery did well before the Second World War, they did even better after the war broke out in 1939. And this was because while most businesses remained in Berlin during the early years of the hostilities, Anton Wenshoffer had the foresight to move the gallery's entire collection from its fashionable premises on the Kurfürstendamm Avenue to an obscurely discreet glass-fronted potting shed on the family's summer estate.

I can't remember the people who made the ten-kilometer journey to this makeshift gallery on the outskirts of the city. Many of the Wenshoffer Gallery's pre-war clientele had left Berlin at the outbreak of war. Or were fighting on the Eastern Front. Or had perished during the Allied air raids. But collectors must have come because every morning my father took a skeleton key from a hook in the entrance hall of our country house, walked across the once-manicured lawn and, at precisely ten o'clock, unlocked the door of the "gallery" in anticipation of meeting a client. Rain or shine, Anton Wenshoffer did this six days a week.

Even more memorable to my five-year-old self was the inferno that engulfed the distant city in the autumn of 1943.

'You'll remember this for the rest of your life, Horst,' my father had told me as he lifted my wiry figure onto his shoulders so that I could get a better view. I never forgot seeing the "fireworks" that reduced Berlin to rubble in three days. Nor, after the Russians entered Berlin two years later, hearing my parents complain about the shortages of food and fuel.

'Hilda, things are worse now than they were during the war.'

I remember hearing, but not exactly understanding, what my prematurely grey-haired mother meant when she talked about the appalling behavior of the Russian soldiers.

'Have you ever wondered why so many of our young women are pretending to have a hideous limp when they walk around town?'

'Or have you noticed how ridiculous the Russian officers look,' my father interjected, 'wearing two gloves and, in keeping with European fashion, carrying a third glove in one hand?'

There is no rubble in the city now, thirty years later. In fact, the only evidence today of the block-to-block fighting that took place during the Soviet army's "liberation" of Berlin in 1945 are the strafe marks that riddle the bottoms of the buildings like gaping wounds. But at the time what happened in the months following the end of the war was no laughing matter.

***

Everyone thought that my father had been *verrückt* to move the art collection back to Berlin when the city was still on its knees. But he hadn't been crazy. The sale of the family's summer residence in 1948 had given him enough money to rebuild the old gallery and to add a spacious high-ceilinged apartment above it. And, since Anton Wenshoffer had not sold all of his stock during the war, when he re-opened the gallery on the Kurfürstendamm in 1949, he had plenty to sell.

And sell he did. He sold to a new generation of collectors who wanted paintings that depicted an era before Kaiser Wilhelm and Adolf Hitler had taken Germany into the First and then into the Second World Wars. He sold to public art-gallery officials who were desperate to fill the gaps in their late-nineteenth-century collections, much depleted by bombardment from Britain's de Havilland Mosquito bombers and Avro Lancasters or "relocated" to Moscow and Leningrad by the Red Army Trophy Brigade. And, after the city had been divided into Russian, American, British and French zones, my father sold to members of the occupying armed forces who lived in the western sector of the city. It seemed that all of them wanted a souvenir to remind them of their posting in war-torn Berlin.

I have only a vague memory of the paintings that father displayed, three rows deep, against the newly painted wine-red walls at the Wenshoffer Gallery's first post-war exhibition. After all, I was only eleven years old in 1949; more interested in collecting American comic books and exploring off-the-limits bomb sites with my friends. But I do remember my statuesque mother sitting, receipt-book in hand, at the elegant Biedermeier desk at the back of the gallery. I also remember the variously coloured uniforms of the military officers. And the shabbily dressed women, bent double under the weight of heavy woollen shawls that added an extra layer of warmth to their threadbare coats. And their German husbands, recently out of uniform, wearing suits that smelled of mothballs.

One moment stands out above all: my father, inevitably the best-dressed man in the room, inviting everyone to meet the future director of the Wenshoffer Gallery. My attempts to avoid being introduced to a throng of strangers as the heir-apparent, by seeking refuge in the storeroom, were in vain. Every ten minutes or so father would find me engrossed in a comic book; then out I'd pop from the storeroom, like an open beaked cuckoo from a Swiss clock, in order to shake hands with a potential client.

The gallery was rarely empty after that first exhibition, even though many of the people who pushed back the glass-fronted door and entered the Wenshoffer Gallery had no intention of buying a picture. Some folks simply sought warmth. Others wanted to be surrounded by the Persian carpets, the red-wine walls and the pictures that reminded them of how they had once lived. Even so, enough people did buy pictures to keep the gallery in the black. And when people purchased nothing, my father insisted that it was good for business if passers-by saw the gallery full of people.

During my first two years of employment at the Wenshoffer Gallery, I hardly needed the fine new suit that Koch and Sons had made for me. Confined to the storeroom, I was rarely in public view. This was because my first job was to record the size, medium, value, title and artist's name — providing I could read the signature — of every work in our vast collection. By the end of two years each picture had its own index card, its own slot in one of the long, floor-to-ceiling storage cabinets that lined the storeroom. And I had developed muscles by lifting the elaborately framed paintings from one storage cabinet to another. My job was made more arduous by my father's insistence that each painting had to be stored in alphabetical order according to the artist's name. This meant re-shelving virtually every work when the gallery acquired a new painting. With so many Berliners offloading their collections before leaving the city in search of a better life elsewhere, there was a lot of lifting and shifting.

The solution to this boring task seemed obvious — to me. I told my father how we could avoid this time-wasting activity by shelving the paintings according to the date that they arrived at the gallery.

'And how will we locate a picture if it isn't placed under the artist's name, Horst?'

My attempts to suggest that every painting could be located, simply by cross-referencing its location on the index cards I'd created for each artist, fell onto deaf ears. After I was promoted from the storeroom to the showroom two years later, I found that my other recommendations met with the same fate.

When I suggested that prospective clients should be allowed to contemplate a painting — and be given enough time to consider how they might pay for it — without having my father, and now me, lurking over their shoulder, I was firmly instructed otherwise.

'Horst, you must greet clients at the front door with a little bow. Then you must accompany them around the gallery, clockwise if possible. And if they hesitate before a work, stand a little to the right of the painting and tell the client something about it. This is the way we've done things since your grandfather opened the gallery.'

'Of course, Father,' was my submissive response. I already sensed that I was up against a deep-seated cultural tradition, stronger than any particular argument I could muster.

I suppose it was during that fitting for my first suit at Koch and Sons that I had been introduced to my fellow countrymen's conviction that there was only one way of doing things — so well characterized by the often-repeated German phrase *Mann muss*, or one must. As Herr Koch measured my over-arm and underarm shoulder width, the length of my long arms and legs and the breadth of my narrow chest, he told me of incidents that gave me some insight into how Koch and Sons had not only survived the Second World War, but had truly prospered.

'Every prisoner in that concentration camp on the outskirts of Berlin, wore one of those broad-striped cotton suits that you have no doubt seen in photographs,' Herr Koch informed me, proudly adding as he laid down the measuring tape, 'and all of them were made by my backroom cutters and sewers.'

This particular camp, which Herr Koch claimed was a few hours' drive to the east of the city, was a mystery — I knew nothing about it. Nor, so it seemed, did anyone else. Was it a transit camp, a prisoner-of-war camp, a forced labor camp? Or was it the gravest detention facility of all, an extermination camp?

I'd seen the blue-and-grey pyjama-like "suits" that prisoners were forced to wear in such camps in the newsreels that ran before every feature film in West Berlin. Reminding Germans about the crimes that had been committed during the *Nazi Zeit* was part of the denazification programme for the country's citizens. Yet the clothing that I saw in the newsreels had no similarity to the tailor-made suits that had made Koch and Sons the finest tailor east of the Rhine. The suits in the newsreels were dirty. The trouser legs resembled stovepipes. The jackets had no breast pocket. And without the benefit of shoulder pads — or of a good meal to fill out the wearer's physique — they resembled recently hung-out washing.

On my second visit to Herr Koch's establishment, the tailor revealed that his firm had not only made the prisoner's uniforms, but that he himself had delivered them to the camp. I thought about this later, and on my final fitting curiosity got the better of me and I asked the tailor to tell me more. Though Herr Koch never revealed the name or the kind of the camp lying so close to Berlin, he did tell me what he had seen on his once-a-week visits.

'I usually made the delivery around seven a.m.,' he began as he held up my new jacket. 'By this time, the prisoners had been standing in front of their barracks since five-thirty a.m. And do you know why I never got home until early evening, Herr Wenshoffer?'

No reply was necessary; he was now mentally reliving the experience.

'If one of the prisoners collapsed from weakness or illness — or simply died during the morning roll call,' he added, wincing at the memory, 'then the commandant, who was responsible for signing my requisition form, had to begin counting the prisoners again. Yes, Herr Wenshoffer, rain or shine, sleet or snow, those poor buggers stood there like pigeons in a shooting gallery.'

Herr Koch paused for a moment to compose himself. Then he held up my jacket once again and I duly slid my arms into the sleeves. He frowned, brushed non-existent lint from my shoulders, took a couple of steps back to admire his handiwork, then retrieved one further, final memory: 'On the day I had to deliver the suits to the camp, I missed my late afternoon coffee and cake.'

***

After my father died in 1963, I became the director of the Wenshoffer Gallery. The idea that "one must" do this or that for no logical reason went out of the door. New acquisitions were shelved in the storeroom cabinets according to when they entered the gallery. Clients were no longer greeted at the door with a little bow or accompanied from one picture to another. Rather, I spent most of my time at the back of the gallery perusing auction catalogues and art magazines. And when I heard the glass door open, I never rose from the Biedermeier desk unless a client walked in my direction and asked for assistance.

While I broke with the rigid order — or, to put it more kindly departed from the way my father and, before him, my grandfather had done things for the previous hundred years — when it came to my personal life, I followed in my parents' footsteps. When I re-decorated the family apartment above the gallery, I retained the early-nineteenth century Biedermeier furnishings. I ate my main meal of the day in the Hotel Kempinsky's elegant dining room, a two-block walk up the Kurfürstendamm. I sent out my washing once a week. I had fresh flowers delivered to my apartment and to the gallery every other day.

I also commissioned Koch and Sons to make me six monographed shirts and two double-breasted suits once every three and a half years. On my one day off a week, I strolled, just as my parents had done before me, under the recently planted linden, chestnut and oak trees in the nearby Tiergarten Park. Then I headed for the Kempinsky tea salon where I treated myself to a slice of cake accompanied by a generous portion of whipped cream. Having been convinced by my mother that all work and no play made Jack a dull boy, I took over the Wenshoffer's private box at the opera house and the Berliner Philharmonic.

I slipped into the privileged lifestyle of my parents all the more easily because, by the early 1970s, the economic miracle that had begun to rebuild the German economy in the 1960s had clearly kicked in. Business was now booming. The Wenshoffer Gallery was turning over a larger profit than during my parents' or even my grandparents' day. I patted myself on the back, putting the gallery's prosperity down to the changes I had made when I became director. Then, quite suddenly, my complacency was punctured. Everyone but me seemed to be driving a Mercedes or a BMW and spending their two-week vacations in the United States or on an island in Greece. Even the city's poorest residents were taking an annual holiday, albeit on a tour bus.

Here was a new style, not only in life but in art: one that might not work to the Wenshoffer Gallery's advantage. Indeed, it seemed that the public art galleries had their quota of late nineteenth century paintings. Their curators were now acquiring only contemporary work. It was said that they were so eager to show that their galleries were up with the times, on the cutting edge of the art scene, that they purchased work before the paint had dried on the canvas. More worrying, the old guard of private collectors, whose desire for paintings with no obvious political or social content had helped the Wenshoffer Gallery prosper during the post-war years, were dying off.

The affluent post-war generation of collectors wanted something different. Paintings that matched the minimalist tube and leather furnishings in their homes. Paintings that filled the large empty spaces between the plate-glass windows in their white-walled office buildings. And above all, they wanted paintings that had nothing to do with the country's past.

At first, I thought that this tide could be resisted. But on second thought I wondered if I had made a mistake by deviating from the unflinching order that my father and grandfather had imposed on the running of the gallery. So, I retreated to their way of doing things. I greeted anyone who entered the gallery with a little bow. When I sensed that the client might have deep pockets, I accompanied them around the gallery — clockwise, of course. If they admired a picture for more than a few seconds, I stood a little to the right of the painting, told them something about the artist before assuring them that, at the price I was asking for the picture, they were assured of a good investment.

Alas, my father's way of doing things proved as unsuccessful as my own. It was time for a radical break. I took new and more drastic measures to keep the Wenshoffer Gallery out of the red. I reduced prices. I broke with family tradition and advertised the gallery in a glossy international art magazine. And I put over half of the pictures in the storeroom on the auction block, subject to reserve prices.

However, few people responded to the advertisement. And the paintings I took to Limpretz's auction house did not meet the reserve. With the view that any sale was better than none, I slashed my prices once again and lowered the reserve. Half of the pictures sold for a song; the others were returned to the storage racks at the back of the gallery.

Lest anyone thought that the Wenshoffer Gallery was about to go out of business, I continued to unlock its glass-fronted door at precisely ten a.m. six days a week. However, behind this façade, I adopted drastic money-saving measures that told another story. I rented the upstairs apartment to a young couple who were thrilled to be living on the fashionable Ku'damm. I now slept at the back of the half-empty storeroom on a camp bed. It was also here that I washed my own shirts and underwear in the small enamel sink next to where I prepared my modest breakfast. When I needed to use a toilet, I skirted around the block and used the facilities at the nearby department store. On Sundays, I resorted to a chamber pot that I kept under my bed. It was emptied in the early hours of Monday morning in a nearby sewage drain.

I ate my main meal of the day at Aushinger's cafeteria, near the zoo train station. There I found that, providing I was willing to share a small chest-high round table and stand with equally down-at-heel people, I could eat two long thin-skinned wieners accompanied by mustard and three bread rolls for a few marks. Conceding that I *had* become a dull boy, I cancelled my subscription to the opera house and the concert hall. When I was lucky enough to sell a painting, I bought a new suit — off the rack. Koch and Sons became a distant memory.

***

Crucially, I still made a daily visit to the Hotel Kempinsky's tea salon, though limiting myself to one glass of tea with citron. And that's where I met Fraülein Mariana Trott.

Now it's not uncommon to speak to a stranger while enjoying a glass of tea in the Hotel Kempinsky's tea salon. It's partly because Berliners like to complain, or *schimpfen*, and because they are not shy to offer their opinion on everything from the weather to the Berlin Wall. Because Berliners are known to have a *grosser klappe* anyone whose head was not buried in a book or a newspaper was deemed to be fair game for a bit of conversation.

With so few customers to talk to at the gallery, I enjoyed hearing the thoughts that bounced around the interior of my mind pop out of my mouth during the hour or so that I spent in Kempinsky's tea salon. I particularly enjoyed conversing with people who knew nothing about the Wenshoffer Gallery's decline and my own dilemma over what to do about it.

Little wonder, then, that I gave a regretful sigh when a young woman with dark curly hair, a ski-jump nose and piercing cobalt-blue eyes looked over to my table and informed me that she had often seen me unlocking the door to the Wenshoffer Gallery. I immediately pulled myself together; after all, she might be a possible client, or have parents who'd be willing to invest in a painting or two. So, I put down my glass of tea, uncrossed my legs, straightened my back, patted the sides of my unfashionably short blond hair and, shifted into art gallery director mode by offering the young woman an invitation: 'Next time you're on the Ku'damm don't just look at the pictures through the window, come into the gallery. I'd be happy to show you around.'

Fraülein Trott made it clear that, as a student at the Free University, her allowance did not stretch to buying works of art. I gave another sigh.

'But that's not to say that I'd refuse your kind offer, Herr Wenshoffer. Actually,' she continued, 'after I graduate next year, I'm planning to open a gallery devoted to contemporary painting and sculpture.'

I refrained from telling the eager young woman that it wouldn't be easy for her to make a living in the commercial art gallery world — unless, of course, she had wealthy parents to back her. Or unless she discovered a young innovative artist, then persuaded the editor of *Deutsche Kunst* to put an image of the artist's work on the cover of their magazine. But even if she struck lucky like this, Fraülein Trott would have to observe less gifted artists flood the market with knock-off copies of *her* artist's work. She would see the value of her artist's work fall; she would watch the gallery's profit margin shrink; and then, after taking a deep breath, she'd spend all of her time finding an artist whose "unique" style would pull her gallery out of debt.

Yet I was hardly in a position to offer advice on how to run a successful art gallery. And I didn't want to dampen the young woman's enthusiasm or miss an opportunity to talk about art, rather than worry about how to sell it. After finishing my tea, I pulled a long out-of-date diary from my breast pocket, hemmed and hawed as I flipped through its empty pages, then, as if suddenly discovering a free day, I tapped my finger on a blank page and made an appointment to show my young acquaintance around the Wenshoffer Gallery.

It turned out to be a day to remember. But it did not begin well. 'Is this all that you've got to show me?' Fraülein Trott asked after she'd spent an hour viewing the twenty or so paintings that hung in one row around the gallery. I answered defensively that I had a few more paintings in the storeroom.

'Could I see those too?'

Confident that my single bed, makeshift wardrobe rack and washstand were concealed behind the last storage cabinet and that I had duly rinsed out my chamber pot, I opened the storeroom door. During the next two hours, I pulled one painting after another from its cubby hole, held it against my chest and, when I sensed that Fraülein Trott had seen enough, put it back in its place. She said little during the impromptu viewing. On the other hand, she showed no signs of boredom or fatigue. In fact, before I could stop her from walking around the final storage cabinet, positioned so as to conceal the reality of my pitiful existence, she was standing right there asking to see more.

'It can't be easy selling these sorts of paintings when everyone is talking about the Neo-Expressionists,' Fraülein Trott said when we were drinking a cup of mint tea in the main gallery after the viewing. 'And it's such a pity because these high ceilings and large windows give your pictures room to breathe. And, as for your location on the Ku'damm, you've got the best venue in the city for an art gallery!'

I knew that my father and grandfather would have agreed, of course — and so did she, quickly adding, in an effort to save my pride: 'There's no doubt that the Wenshoffer Gallery continues to remain the top private art gallery in West Berlin.'

There it was, I reflected, after my young acquaintance left a few minutes later. Out of the mouths of babes comes the truth. Fraülein Trott's reference to contemporary art had been a subtle way of commenting on the kind of paintings that had hung on the walls and been stored in the back room of the Wenshoffer Gallery for a century. However, they were now, in 1970s West Berlin, old-hat, facile — little more than clichéd examples of late-nineteenth century bourgeois culture.

I'd never considered any of the paintings in the Wenshoffer Gallery to be out of tune with the times. Sure, they had been created before I was born. But so had the ever-popular Impressionist and Post-Impressionist paintings that still commanded high prices and much interest.

The reality was that I'd long taken comfort from the idyllic scenes the paintings depicted. During the bombing of Berlin when, perched on my father's shoulders, I had watched the "fireworks" from a safe distance. During the post-war years when everyone was forced to take responsibility for the terrible things that had happened during the war. During the airlift in 1948 to 1949 when I and my fellow West Berliners were kept alive — and awake during the night — by the broad-bellied transport aircraft that delivered food and fuel to a city that was cut off from the west by the Russians.

Surely other people, I thought, must have taken similar comfort from the kinds of pictures that were the Wenshoffer Gallery's stock and trade. Or at least I had thought that until Fraülein Trott had so candidly indicated that the art scene in Germany had moved well beyond the sentimental paintings that gave me such pleasure — and all too few sales. In fact, until meeting her, I'd never given much thought to contemporary art.

During the following week, however, I borrowed trendy art magazines from the local library and studied their contents. And I visited a makeshift warehouse gallery on the other side of town. What I read and saw revealed that a new generation of artists, whom the art critics called the Neo-Expressionists, were attempting to build a new cultural legacy for Germany. And they were doing this by giving little attention to form or to detail. By applying what could only be called gaudy colours to their raw canvases. By distorting their figures.

And by eliminating any vestige of sentimentality from their work. The Neo-Expressionists were not only turning the figures in their paintings on their heads. They were turning away from tradition, indeed turning away from all of those things that I so much admired in the few remaining late-nineteenth century paintings that hung on the walls of the Wenshoffer Gallery.

***

When I caught sight of Mariana Trott at the Hotel Kempinsky five days later, she wasn't alone. Two young men, dressed in jeans and paint-splattered tee-shirts, shared her small round table. They not only looked out of place, they looked uncomfortable. Yet the way they kept glancing towards my table made me think that they had come to the tea salon with an ulterior purpose. They were certainly talking about me because I heard them mention my name more than once.

Mariana, as I was soon to call her, was too well-mannered to mock anyone who was within hearing distance. So, I didn't think that they could be saying anything bad about me. In fact, when Mariana raised her arm and waved me over to her table, and the young men shifted their seats in order to make room for another chair, then stood up to be introduced when I approached, I knew that I had indeed been the subject of their conversation.

173

Manfred Stoff and Walter Kass were both artists. The revelation that they shared a studio on the top floor of an abandoned warehouse in the working-class district of Kreuzberg should have warned me that they were part of the Neo-Expressionist brigade. Mariana now wasted no time in setting out her agenda.

'You know as well as we do how precious gallery space is in West Berlin. And I think you also know from what I said during our meeting last week that, although you've got the best venue in town, the kind of art you're selling is not exactly at the cutting edge of the art market.'

I did not need to be told, for a second time in a week, that Mariana considered the Wenshoffer Gallery to be passé — "out of sync", as people now said — and above all, that the paintings hanging on my walls hardly reflected the schizophrenic city that history and politics had sliced in two. I pushed back my chair and was about to stand up and politely bid the young people good afternoon when Mariana put her hand on my arm and adroitly added, 'Personally, Herr Wenshoffer, I respect your gallery's long and distinguished history. But the public now wants a new kind of art.'

Wearing we-told-you-so expressions on their faces, and apparently wanting to be anywhere else but at the Hotel Kempinsky's tea salon, Manfred and Walter looked in every direction except towards me. Undaunted, Mariana tilted her nose into the air, took a deep breath, then asked if I would allow her to curate an exhibition at the Wenshoffer Gallery featuring Walter and Manfred's most recent paintings.

"Their work *is* on the cutting edge, Herr Wenshoffer. And, given the right sort of exposure afforded by an exhibition at your marvellous gallery, I am confident that their paintings would sell.'

I sat down and took a closer look at Manfred and Walter. What I saw were two artists, on the brink of their careers, desperate for an opportunity to show their work. Indeed, they were both hungry for the kind of opportunity that had been handed to me on a silver platter when I began my apprenticeship in the Wenshoffer Gallery's storeroom.

I suppose I could think in this way because — until recently — I never had to worry about meeting costs at the end of the month. Or think about how to draw clients into the gallery. Or wonder where I might eat a cheap meal or surreptitiously dispose the waste from my chamber pot in the early hours of the morning. In fact, the faces of the young men who had accompanied Mariana to the tea salon belied a look not only of desperation but of resignation. It was an expression that I'd recently come to know. I saw it on my own face every morning when I looked into the mirror to shave.

So, I now took a deep breath, glanced towards Mariana, and simply blurted out: 'Why not?'

My three new acquaintances cheered. The waiters and regular customers, who only knew me as the prosperous though somewhat taciturn gallery director, raised their eyebrows in surprise. However, if anyone was surprised, it was me.

Because, only a week earlier, I'd dismissed the few examples of Neo-Expressionist painting that I'd seen in the fine-art magazines and on the walls of emerging galleries around the city. I had no experience of dealing with living artists simply because the paintings that I sold had all been created by artists who were long dead. Yet, in an unguarded moment, I had agreed to allow the Wenshoffer Gallery to host an exhibition of Neo-Expressionist art. Agreed to let Mariana Trott decide which pictures to include in the projected exhibition. And, above all, agreed to permit her, Manfred and Walter, to transform my gallery from a facsimile of a late-nineteenth century middle-class living room into a white cube. And I would now have to face the consequences.

***

During the weeks that followed, I watched Mariana and her friends strip the wine-red paper off the walls of the Wenshoffer Gallery. They now replaced it with plaster boards which they painted matt white. I winced as they lowered the gallery's three elegant chandeliers, so proudly installed by my father for the gallery's opening in 1949. Instead, they attached a combination of flood and spotlights to the ceiling. They saw to it that a much-needed toilet was installed in the storeroom (and I was happy to throw away the chamber pot). Finally, Manfred and Walter spat on their hands, lifted the heavy Biedermeier desk and carried it into the storeroom. Three leather and stainless steel Brauer Wassily chairs, on loan from the newly opened Bauhaus Museum, were placed at the end of a gallery.

Two days before the exhibition opened, I had had good reason to question the sanity of my 'Why not?' response, when Manfred and Walter carried twelve canvases into the gallery. I hadn't prepared myself for the sheer size of the work, nor for what they depicted. Rendered in the Neo-Expressionist style, they could only be described as chaotic, unsymmetrical, and lacking any sense of order. And, as for the colours: they were either muddy or gaudy. No wonder I could not imagine that anyone would be interested in viewing, let alone in buying any of these disturbing paintings.

It was Mariana who had insisted on calling the exhibition *Why Not?* On the opening night, a sandwich board displaying the title of the show and the names of the two young artists was placed in the centre on the wide sidewalk. (Of course, the Wenshoffer Gallery had never before stooped so low as to advertise on the pavement.) Wanting to be anywhere but in my own gallery, I treated myself to a meal in the Hotel Kempinsky's belle époque dining room. Sitting under a four-tiered crystal chandelier, I lingered over my wine; I smoked a cigar and ended my meal with a large glass of cognac. Then, preparing for humiliation and defeat, I left.

Even before I reached the gallery, I could hear David Bowie's hit-tune *Heroes* that he'd recorded at the Hansa Studio in Berlin two years earlier. And when I got closer, I could see that a large crowd had spilled onto the sidewalk. It seemed that the Wenshoffer Gallery was chock-a-block full. Indeed, so full that in order to gain entry, I was forced to shout: 'Let me through, I'm the director, I'm Horst Wenshoffer.'

And the people I pushed aside as I headed towards the back of the gallery were not, as I had anticipated, all long-haired and sloppily dressed students and artists. There were well-heeled businessmen on the lookout for a painting to decorate their apartment or office. There were smartly dressed younger couples who were about to acquire their first painting. Few of these people were much older than myself.

No one, with the single exception of a middle-aged woman who caught a glimpse of what was left of my nineteenth century collection when using the toilet, was interested in the kind of pictures that had once made the Wenshoffer Gallery famous. Even that worked out well for me: anticipating that these nostalgic works might eventually come back into fashion, the woman made an appointment to view them the following week and, after only a few minutes, she offered to buy the lot. Now assured that I was about to make a modest profit, I agreed, holding back just a dozen or so of my favourite pictures.

I should have had more faith in my young friends. The opening was an event, an immediate success. Everyone looked happy and appeared excited by what they were viewing. A young photographer, representing one of Germany's leading art magazines, asked when she could set up her equipment for a photoshoot.

'Any morning next week before the gallery opens at ten a.m. is fine with me,' I told her without going through the motions of consulting my empty diary, still lodged in the breast pocket of my outdated Koch and Sons double-breasted suit.

A little later, I heard the same photographer telling Manfred and Walter: 'No, your paintings won't appear on the cover of the magazine, but they'll be given plenty of space inside it.' The young artists were nevertheless clearly overjoyed to receive this kind of attention for their first exhibition. And newspaper journalists were present too. They interviewed Walter and Manfred. They sought a pithy quotation from the curator of the show, Mariana Trott. And a woman with spikey jet-black hair even sought me out.

'Whatever prompted you to depart from the Wenshoffer Gallery's long-standing tradition of selling late nineteenth paintings and move into field of contemporary art, Herr Wenshoffer?'

I could afford to evade the young woman's question because the answer was already apparent:

every painting in the show had a glittering red star indicating that it had been sold. I literally saw stars myself as I turned my back on the reporter, then pushed my way through the crowd towards the front of the gallery. I opened the glass-fronted door and stepped outside.

It was a bitterly cold evening. I had no overcoat or hat to protect me as I made my way up the Ku'damm. I walked past the Hotel Kempinsky and the Cinema Paris. I walked through Lihnerner and Henrietten Platz with their expensive shops. I walked and walked and walked until I reached the inner ring road at the end of the Kurfürstendamm. Then I stopped, bent over and retched.

It wasn't the cold weather that had transformed me into one of the distorted figures in Walter's paintings. I could sense that the drivers, whose headlights illuminated my bent-over figure, thought that I was just another drunk. Of course, I wasn't drunk. I was dead sober. And I wasn't even cold. I was heaving my guts out because I saw that the old world, the world of my father and my grandfather before him, had no place in German society.

No one wanted to imaginatively join the frolicking Bavarian peasants for a drink in the beer garden, or to accompany the bourgeois family on their seaside vacation, or to listen in on what the maid was hearing from the open door, or to lose themselves in one of those late nineteenth century mist-filled alpine landscape paintings. Even I couldn't do these things, because the

Wenshoffer Gallery was jam-packed with paintings that challenged the conformism and order, along with the must-do mentality, that my beloved late nineteenth century paintings represented. What people now wanted were paintings that confronted the dark side of German history head-on. Paintings that pointed a finger at everyone — from the tailor, Herr Koch, to the commandant of the concentration camp and even to my own father, who had profited from the refugees who had been forced to offload their collections at the Wenshoffer Gallery before fleeing from the Nazis.

It must have been two a.m. by the time I returned to the gallery. Marianne, Manfred and Walter were still there. 'We didn't have a key so thought we'd better wait for you to return.' They had removed and washed the wine glasses, they had swept the floor and they were now attempting to turn the Breuer Wassily chairs into beds. They had taken charge.

***

After that private view in January 1979 no one ever again associated the Wenshoffer Gallery with late-nineteenth century painting. Instead, it became a leading centre of Neo-Expressionist art, not just in Berlin, or only in Germany, but around the world.

It's easy to supply a fairy tale ending to the story. You can easily imagine that, following her graduation, Mariana Trott joined the Wenshoffer Gallery, leaving me free to visit artists in their studios, in their lofts and in their warehouses. That it was me who represented the Wenshoffer Gallery's bright young contemporary artists at Kassel's *Documenta* and at Venice's *Biennale*. That, after the wall came down in 1989, it was me who mounted an exhibition devoted to the graffiti artists who had painted the west side of the wall that had previously divided East and West Berlin. That it was me who fulfilled a lifetime ambition to visit New York City by lending paintings by our best artists to the Museum of Modern Art's first show devoted to the Neo-Expressionist art. That it was me who was hailed as a champion of Germany's contemporary artists, and me who was often described as the city's most eligible bachelor. And that, in the natural progression of things, it was me who ended such flattering speculation when I married Mariana Trott.

This is, indeed, how my forty-year-old self would have liked the story to have unfolded after our seminal exhibition on a cold wintery night in 1979. But things turned out differently. Mariana did work for the Wenshoffer Gallery; but she didn't marry me, she married Walter. And it was Manfred, not me, who became the gallery's impresario — and the city's most sought-after gay bachelor.

True, my new-found wealth did allow me to reclaim my apartment above the gallery. I could again eat my main meal of the day at the Hotel Kempinsky whenever I wished (though, to hedge my bet against fate,

I still ate two wieners and three buns at Aushingers once a week). I could indeed now afford to commission Koch and Sons to make my tailor-made double-breasted suits and monographed shirts — but I chose instead to buy my suits off the rack and to purchase my shirts from the department store around the corner. I did send out my washing and I ordered flowers for the gallery twice a week. I also chose to renew my annual subscription to the Berliner Philharmonic and Opera House.

And above all, I remain the titular head of the Wenshoffer Gallery. Though I unlock the glass-fronted door at precisely ten a.m. every morning I spend less time in the gallery. My staff know where to find me if they need a cheque signed or the rent paid. I'll be upstairs in my apartment, surrounded by Biedermeier furniture from another era; taking comfort from the works of art that hang on its walls — those images in the dozen or so late nineteenth century paintings that once made the Wenshoffer Gallery the talk of the town, and which I myself chose to rescue. Why not?

Metamorphosis

I entered the world as a shell. When I gave up that life, I joined thousands of other marine invertebrates at the bottom of a warm, shallow sea and turned into limestone. After the sea had dried up and the heat and the pressure from the earth's crust had metamorphosed me into marble, I found myself living in a mountain five thousand feet above sea level.

I was fortunate to have had this second incarnation in the world's finest deposit of marble. Fortunate also that the Ancient Romans turned Carrara's Luna marble into paving stones, into friezes and even into statues that became prized artefacts of their civilization. I was fortunate, too, that there was plenty of marble left in the early sixteenth century. That's when an artist known to posterity as Michelangelo had visited the quarry below the mountain where I lived and had roughed out a six-meter-high sculpture called *David*.

I was not only fortunate that mere marble had become the preferred material for high art during the Renaissance. Two centuries later, when a renewed interest in ancient Greek and Roman sculpture gave rise to the Neoclassical movement, I was given a new life. Of course, artistic movements come and go, but marble is forever. And I was lucky to be made of the right stuff and living in the right place at the right time when artistic styles and tastes changed once again.

It was towards the end of the Neoclassical era that a quarry worker had the courage to suspend himself halfway down the face of my mountain. He drilled, then he hammered several wet wooden wedges into the area where I lived. And then he waited. When the wedges had dried, the five-ton block of marble where I lived cracked. It separated from the high marble wall. And I fell to the ground.

For me, my release from the mountain turned out to be good fortune. But it was less fortunate for the two men who were working at the bottom of the quarry. As they squared off my block using a two-handed saw, they risked being sent to an early death by inhaling the marble chips and dust. And because they continued to work during the hottest hours of the day, they risked blindness from the glare of the sun.

For me, however, there were no such risks. I was lucky that a team of oxen had the muscle to pull my hefty block of marble along the dirt track that linked the quarry to the port of Avenza. This is where I was loaded on to a flat-bottomed barge then transferred to an offshore vessel that took me through the Tyrrhenian Sea to the port of Ostia. It was from here that I was triumphantly barged fifteen kilometers up the Tiber River to Rome and subsequently delivered into the hands of Europe's most celebrated sculptor.

***

In 1787 Antonio Canova had made a name for himself by creating a funerary monument for the tomb of Pope Clement XIV. By the time I arrived at his workshop over thirty years later, Canova was in his mid-fifties and his Neoclassical sculptures were much in demand. Some of his patrons commissioned edifying mythological figures. Others, among whom were popes and princes, empresses and queens, wanted images of themselves garbed in Ancient Roman or Greek robes. Such was Canova's fame that he was invited to make a sculpture of America's first president, George Washington, and not one but two of Napoleon Bonaparte.

Initially, I shared one of the seven rooms comprising Canova's imposing residence with several other blocks of marble. The vast chamber was a sort of holding shed: a no man's land where we all waited to have an identity thrust upon us by the great sculptor. I didn't have to wait here long before I was liberated from my block because it seemed that every serious collector wanted to own a marble statue by Antonio Canova. Certainly, this is why an Englishman by the name of John Russell, formally known as the sixth Duke of Bedford, had visited the sculptor's *studio grande* on his tour of Europe in the early years of the nineteenth century.

John Russell knew what he wanted when he walked into Canova's showroom. Disdainfully, he ignored the portrait busts, marble friezes and life-sized statues that jostled for space — and for the attention of any prospective buyer. The duke had just seen an engraving of Canova's marble statue, *The Three Graces,* depicting Zeus's three daughters of charity. And, although Canova had already produced two sculptures of the three maidens, the duke wanted the famous sculptor to make him a third version. He had even chosen the place where *The Three Graces* would be displayed: the largest, most stately room in his country house at Woburn Abbey.

Canova had no difficulty accepting the commission. The charcoal drawings along with the three-dimensional *bonzzetti* or clay sketches and the full-scale plaster casts from the two previous sculptures of *The Three Graces* would serve as a reference point for this new work. So would the stylistic conventions of Neoclassical sculpture. Thus, the three maidens in the new work would be elegant and idealized. They would be expressionless and sexless. And they would possess a monumental stillness reminiscent of Ancient Greek and Roman sculpture. Even so, Canova wanted to do more than replicate his two previous sculptures. Rather than depicting the three maidens in a huddled embrace, Canova intended to represent them as independent figures. They would have outstretched arms and individual expressions. And if the duke didn't like this modified version of *The Three Graces*, Canova knew that he'd have no trouble selling it to someone else.

Almost as soon as John Russell had left the *studio grande* I was moved to a large, high-ceilinged room. Here, two men known as pointers used long-handled steel calipers to measure my block against the plaster model that Canova had made for his new work. Next, two other men, wielding bull-headed mallets and blunt chisels, gave me one blow per second. Every blow made me shudder as it reverberated through my marmoreal encasement. After the men had roughed out my block to the point where I resembled a meringue blanche, I was wheeled into a large studio.

This is when I met Antonio Canova face to face. This is where "the supreme minister of beauty", as the sculptor was known, would transform me into an object of beauty, thereby endowing me with an aesthetic significance that would successively shape and reshape my identity.

Over the next several weeks Antonio Canova began a work of liberation that would ultimately allow me to find myself — though not quite as the sculptor first intended. Cutting at an oblique angle with fine comb-like tooth chisels, rasps and riffers, Canova abstracted more weight from my three maidens. Working by candlelight, he gave delicate shading to every crevice of their bodies. Then he polished me with soft pieces of leather. And, inspired by the recent discovery that the Greeks had actually painted their marble sculptures, he began to rub me with a mixture of grind-water and wax so that my three maidens would have a yellow glow that resembled human flesh. Alas, the famous sculptor did not complete this final stage of the work.

I heard the crack several seconds before Antonio Canova fully comprehended what had happened.

During the following days, there was much discussion as to why, after Canova had worked on my marble block for less than a month, it had split into three pieces. Some said that my block was flawed. Others claimed that the pointers had produced crucially inaccurate measurements; certainly, they now found themselves without a job. Still others claimed that the men who had been given the task of roughing me out had not fully appreciated how inflexible and how stubbornly resistant marble can be. Almost everybody got some of the blame; but naturally no one had the audacity to suggest, directly at least, that it was Canova who had lost his touch. Or that the sculptor should have known that rendering the three maidens with outstretched arms was beyond the low tensile strength of the material — in fact, beyond what my particular block of marble could deliver. Anyway, Canova would now have to look elsewhere for another block to replace mine.

***

189

I suppose I was lucky that the three pieces of my failed and discarded sculpture were not simply crushed or broken into paving stones. Rather, the remnants of my "three disgraces" were taken back to the holding shed and dropped in a corner.

I had clearly fallen into bad company, with a reputation besmirched by failure. My future prospects looked dismal until, quite unexpectedly, Canova received an unusual commission from his friend, the long-widowed Count Eugenio Simoni.

The Tuscan banker, who lived in a palazzo in a fashionable area of Lucca, did not want to commission Canova to make him a sculpture of a classical figure nor a portrait bust of himself but instead an image of his daughter, Giovanna, who had died at the age of twelve. Count Simoni didn't want anything grand. 'The sculpture must not exceed the height of a ceramic wine vessel,' he told Canova, 'nor should you clothe her figure in the discreet robes of death.' These instructions were already quite specific, restrictive even. 'And whatever you do Canova,' the banker called out over his shoulder as he left the showroom, 'don't depict Giovanna in that androgynous, cold and lifeless Neoclassical style.'

Antonio Canova had never met Giovanna Simoni, who had died a year earlier when the Asiatic cholera plague swept through Europe. Thus, creating a realistic head-to-toe commemorative sculpture of the young woman should have been impossible. But, as luck would have it, just weeks before the twelve-year-old girl had fallen ill and died, the count had commissioned a miniature portrait of his favorite daughter. It still survives, highly prized, highly priced if it were ever sold. And this is what Simoni now gave to Canova as a guide.

In it, Giovanna wears a high-waisted, loosely-fitting, periwinkle-blue chemise with a short, fitted, single-breasted jacket. Her pitch-black hair is parted in the center and tight ringlets fall over her ears. All of this was in keeping with the restrained and formal Neoclassical style. Yet in other respects the miniature portrait transgresses such conventions. For Giovanna's breasts are full and sensuous — some would say improbably large for a girl of her age. Her smile is on the verge of breaking into a laugh. And her coquettish gaze suggests a visceral engagement with the artist who had once painted her portrait.

The miniature artist's departure from the Neoclassical style were not lost on Canova. Nor was the challenge of creating an artistic representation in stone of what was already an artist's representation in watercolor on ivory. In fact, the beguiling image of Giovanna impelled Canova to attempt something entirely different. He would portray the young maiden in the nude. In doing this he would make no preparatory drawings or clay sketches; nor instruct his assistants to do the work of roughing out the marble in preparation for his final touch or *ultima manor*. Instead, Canova would select a suitably small piece of marble from the holding shed, return to his studio and carve directly into the marble himself.

As the smallest piece of marble among the three disgraces, I again found my future determined for me. Using the miniature portrait as his guide, Canova gave me a sensuous mouth and full breasts, with my nude figure in a relaxed pose. And, just to show that marble could be as flexible as butter in the hands of a genius, the sculptor extended my arms in supplication. Or did the pose suggest that I was inviting the artist, who had painted the miniature portrait of Giovanna, to embrace the body that Canova was about to depict in stone?

What is clear is that I was not transformed into a larger-than-life classical assemblage of *The Three Maidens* as initially planned. Now, I was anything but grand. Measuring just over twelve inches high, I was smaller than any of Canova's previous sculptures. Moreover, because I was destined to live in a private residence rather than in the palace of a prince or in the country house of a duke, I would be unknown to the public at large. Nonetheless, I would be unique. One of a kind. Special.

***

In such ways I lived up to the sculptor's ambitions and intentions. Then fate intervened to seal my uniqueness, for I turned out to be the last work that Canova completed before his death in 1822. I was again a survivor, albeit in a changed form.

Henceforth I sat on a Corinthian-crested plinth in the main reception room of Count Simoni's handsome palazzo. When everyone, from the scullery maid to the count himself, passed through the room they caressed my body. And when the sweat and grime from their hands turned my breasts and buttocks brown, I was subjected to a good scrubbing with a poultice of baking soda and water. But I was more than the focus of attention for this prosperous banker and his retinue. I was an icebreaker. I noticed that awkward visitors lowered their voices and became more willing to converse in my presence. And, in addition to this, I was also now a traveler, a commuter of sorts.

During the summer months, when the heat in Lucca became unbearable, Count Simoni exchanged his tight-fitting corset, his knee-length breeches and silk stockings for a shapeless, loose-fitting garment. I was removed from my plinth, packed into a wooden box filled with soft hay and transported to a stylish but unpretentious villa in the hills above Bagni di Lucca. For three months of every year, I sat on a stone window ledge overlooking the Serchio Valley. During that time, the rays of the sun made me as hard as a diamond.

This see-sawing between Lucca itself and the villa ended in 1835. That was the year when Count Simoni fell out of favor with the Grand Duchy of Tuscany officials for supporting Giuseppe Garibaldi and his followers who wanted to make the Italian Peninsula into a united and democratic country. And a year after that, when the count had meanwhile escaped to France, I was returned to my wooden box and stored in the cool vault of the Simoni bank in Lucca. There I remained until well after Garibaldi created the Kingdom of Italy in 1871.

By this time, Count Eugenio Simoni was dead. His family, who had been scattered during the years of political exile, gradually returned to Lucca. Simoni's grandchildren had a vague sense that I signified something important to them when they restored me to my plinth, but had forgotten which member of the family I represented and who had created me. In fact, in 1890 following a cursory inspection by the next generation now well-established in Lucca, they returned me to the vault. And I did not find a settled place in the Simoni household again until 1922. That was the year that King Victor Emmanuel invited Benito Mussolini to form a new government. The year that Italy's new prime minister called upon Italy's sculptors to create an art that was "traditionalist and modernist at the same time".

Stylistically both classical and contemporary, I was not only a fitting pin-up girl for the newly elected regime; I became the Simoni family's insurance policy against the unpredictable Fascist Party and its leader, Mussolini. Thus, they opportunely removed me from the vault, scrubbed me until I was as white as the sculptures of homoerotic athletes that encircled Rome's

Foro Mussolini stadium and returned me to my plinth in the palazzo.

Now the Simoni family were Sephardic Jews. Their Jewishness had posed no problem during the early years of the Second World War, which Mussolini had joined in 1940 when Hitler's Germany was riding high. But after the fall of the Italian dictator and the landing of the Allied forces on the Italian peninsula in 1943, the Simoni family became apprehensive of their own position. This was especially true when they found themselves living within the German defense line that snaked through the northern Apennine mountains.

The Simoni family thus had the ill luck to be residing in their summer residence in the autumn of 1943. That was when Jews, foreigners and others deemed to be "undesirable" were rounded up by German soldiers in the middle of the night and taken to the collection point at the Hotel delle Terme in Bagni di Lucca. In the process, every member of the Simoni household was transported to Milan, then shipped like cattle to one of the notorious extermination camps in Germany. Tragically, there were no survivors. My own fate was fortuitously different.

***

The Simoni villa was unlocked when Chaplain Stanley Ames pushed his shoulder against the heavy oak door. The chaplain found me sitting on the stone window ledge just inside the front door. I was exactly what he wanted.

It wasn't just the Germans who looted during the Second World War. Every soldier wanted a badge, a cap, a Luger handgun, a Leica camera or, if they had the guts to unpin it from the uniform of a dead German soldier, an iron cross. Chaplain Stanley Ames had little taste for acquiring war booty of this sort. Even so, he should have handed me over to the British and American Monuments officers who were charged with repatriating the works of art they found as they travelled up and down the boot of Italy. But how was the chaplain to know that I was the work, indeed the final work, of Italy's most famous sculptor? Stanley Ames's motives were far more commonplace.

He had promised his young daughter that he'd bring her something back from his "travels". He'd found nothing suitable when the 3rd Infantry Brigade, for whom he was chaplain, had fought their way through North Africa, invaded Sicily, then, crossing the Straits of Messina, had landed on the Italian peninsula.

But when Captain Ames climbed the hill behind Bagni di Lucca that day in the autumn of 1944 to escape the heat and humidity in the valley, he had found exactly what he was looking for. He put me between his sweaty hairy chest and his scratchy army uniform. And when he returned to his quarters, I was snuggled between the clothing and framed photograph of his wife and daughter that made his canvas hold-all look like an unexploded bomb.

The hold-all was smelly compared to my hay-scented wooden box. But I was well protected against the knocks, thumps and bumps that I endured as the chaplain and his regiment fought their way through Italy; then later as they were deployed in Belgium and Holland and finally saw VE Day in Hamburg, Germany. At last, after these wearily prolonged travails across Europe, Chaplain Ames and I finally boarded a ship bound for Portsmouth. I was now far from home, with a provenance that was as uncertain as my future prospects.

I wasn't a hit when the reverend, on reaching his home and family, presented me to his daughter Kate, now seven years old. 'She's so hard; not soft like my other dolls.'

My marble was not the only problem, as Stanley's wife Clara quickly pointed out: 'The image of a young naked girl is hardly a fitting ornament for a vicar of the Church of England to possess, let alone to display.'

To avoid embarrassment, I was discreetly placed behind a family portrait that adorned the roughly hewn wooden mantel above the fireplace. Seen now as naked rather than nude, I remained there until January 1947. That was the year that an anti-cyclone from Sweden brought large drifts of snow and low temperatures to England. The year that animals froze to death, schools were closed and the electricity was rationed to a few hours a day. The farmers in the Reverend Stanley

Ames's Suffolk parish suffered greatly and his daughter Kate missed two months of school. Everyone and everything in the Ames's vicarage froze, including me. Perhaps this is why Kate felt I needed covering.

Now material was scarce during the Second World War. Women were told to "make do and mend". Young Kate had watched her nimble-fingered mother transform curtains, sheets and blankets into dresses, trousers and even into underwear. And material was still in short supply after the war had ended. Nevertheless, Kate found the remnant of a flannel sheet and by the time the temperatures had risen and rain had replaced snow in March 1947, I was presented to Kate's school friends wearing a dress.

My outstretched arms, my beautifully proportioned figure and my pleasant beguiling expression had provided my young seamstress with a perfect mannequin. By the time Kate was twelve, she'd made me several broad-shouldered suits and pairs of wide-legged trousers. She'd even made me a cocky hat with a net veil and a fur tippet which she draped over my shoulders.

When Kate celebrated her sixteenth birthday, I was wearing brightly patterned, tight-waisted dresses with scratchy crinolines. I had a strapless bathing suit which showed enough décolleté to prompt Reverend Ames to look at me twice when his daughter presented the result of an afternoon's hard work to her father.

Although Kate got some of her ideas from *Harpers*, *Vanity Fair* and *Vogue* fashion magazines, most of the designs for my growing wardrobe came from her own imagination.

Such was Kate's skill as a seamstress and potential fashion designer that when she left high-school in the mid-1950s she refused to follow the usual route for a vicar's daughter of earning a teaching certificate, qualifying as a nurse or going to one of the women's colleges at Oxford or Cambridge Universities. All that Kate wanted to do was to design clothes. So, thanks to her forward-looking parents and to her father's connection with a former sergeant who'd become one of Britain's most distinguished Savile Row tailors, Kate and I left the vicarage in Suffolk and moved down to London.

Kate spent five years learning how to stitch and cut; to repair and alter; and how to measure a male client without blushing when she asked: 'How do you dress, sir?' During her spare time — which wasn't much given her long hours — I served as Kate's mannequin. Thus, by the early 1960s I was wearing well-above-the-knee dresses made out of gingham, poplin and even from vinyl. When my ready-to-wear wardrobe was complete, Kate took me and my clothes to a boutique fashion designer on the King's Road. She proudly dressed me in one and then another of her new creations. The owners of the boutique liked what they saw and Kate was hired as a junior designer on the spot.

Kate now seemed to be on her way to recognition as one of the top fashion designers in Great Britain. Indeed, by the time London had surpassed Paris as the center of European fashion in the late 1960s, Kate had opened her own fashion boutique and I was moved from her modest bedsit to her new shop. I had served as her mannequin; but it was unclear if I could be accepted as her mascot.

'I see you've brought a souvenir back from your recent trip to Italy,' was the kind of remark that people made when they saw me poised in all of my splendid nakedness on the edge of Kate's teak desk. 'No,' came an improvised response, 'I found her in a junk shop when I was visiting my parents in Suffolk a few weekends ago.' And this, like it or not, was the identity that was thrust upon me. I was no longer given due reverence as a work of art, but simply regarded by most people who bothered to give me a second look, as a curious piece of junk that someone had got rid of for a few pounds.

***

Kate's offhand reply, her improvised cover-up, seemed to satisfy everyone's curiosity — at least until her new beau walked into her office for the first time in the early 1970s. A curator in the sculpture department at the Victoria and Albert Museum, John Clare didn't have to look at me twice to realize that I had an aesthetic standing of a different order altogether — indeed that I might well have been fashioned by a master of Italian sculpture. He went away to do his homework. I was compared with the other Italian Neoclassical sculptures at the Victoria and Albert Museum. Then, following his hunch that I might be the work of Antonio Canova, the young curator travelled to Italy.

John Clare was now asking the right questions, so it was highly likely that he would come up with the right answers. After consulting Canova's records in Rome and Venice, he duly retrieved the story of when and for whom I had been created.

My forgotten history was now my provenance. After that, I was no longer a war trophy or a mannequin. I was a work of art, and a great work of art at that. And surely, like all masterpieces, I no longer belonged solely to Kate, but to the world. Or did I? It was an issue that would need to be resolved.

After John Clare had returned from Italy, I was put on display in the sculpture hall at the Victoria and Albert Museum. But Kate missed me as an object so redolent of her childhood, that I found myself back on her desk. I sat there for another year. I could tell that Kate's beau had not lost interest in me, any more than he had done in Kate. In fact, the couple had meanwhile become engaged.

It was some time after their engagement that John Clare announced that he was to become a contributing curator to an exhibition devoted to the sculpture of

Antonio Canova. Organized by a group of American scholars with a promised opening at the Metropolitan Museum in New York, this was obviously a great career opportunity for the young English curator — and for me too.

Kate was both pleased and distressed. She was torn between her loyalty to John Clare and to her father. The arguments for and against including me in the Canova exhibition went on around me, literally over my head. John assured my reluctant owner that I'd be given star billing at the exhibition, which Kate did not doubt, though nor did she welcome its implications. Then there was the publicity, which John clearly wished to court and Kate to shun. He insisted that being included in the Canova exhibition would increase my value, with a favorable impact on Kate's bank account. 'But what about the cost of insurance should I decide to keep it?' Kate asked him.

Equally, Kate feared that my newly discovered provenance would attract attention to the Simoni family's horrific demise at Auschwitz. Then there was my mysterious arrival in England. Kate knew this would raise all sorts of questions. She could well imagine an investigative journalist, who spotted a good story in the making, pressing her for answers — had she really bought me for a few quid in a junk shop, and if so, where? And what if the reporter were to dig deeper and discover that Kate's own father, the now retired Reverend Ames, was in the relevant part of Italy at just the time that the Simoni villa had been looted?

Despite all of her misgivings, Kate finally bowed to the wishes of her fiancé. And this is how I came to be placed in a sea of Styrofoam in a pale blue box stamped with the number, 5885.

I crossed the Atlantic on a first-class ticket. I had a seat of my own right next to my attentive courier, John Clare. We were met in New York by a cavalcade of motorcycled policeman who, sirens blazing, ushered our bullet-proof limousine from John F Kennedy Airport to the back door of the Metropolitan Museum of Art. John signed a lot of papers, then handed me over to the director of the museum who gave me to a white-gloved handler. In John's presence, the handler checked me over for any damage, then placed me in the center of a temperature-controlled, dimly lit, plexiglass box.

Two hours later I found myself in the museum's sculpture court where I was surrounded by no fewer than twenty of Antonio Canova's sculptures. Leningrad's Hermitage Museum had lent the Met their copy of *The Three Graces*. The plaster model of George Washington was on show courtesy of the Frick Collection in New York City. (The original marble sculpture had been destroyed in a fire a few years after it had arrived in America in the 1830s.) There were several sculptures of nymphs including the Louvre's *Cupid and Psyche*. The curators had even managed to persuade the Accademia di Belle Arti in Venice to lend them Canova's right hand. This rather grisly object was concealed in a small casket. No one could see it. But everyone knew that Canova's right hand, which had taken on the aura of a saintly relic, was in the box.

I was star attraction of the show. My image appeared on posters, on coffee mugs and on tee-shirts. I was illustrated on the cover of the catalogue. And I got the longest entry in the catalogue. In it, John Clare claimed that I represented "the bridge between copying and seeing; between aesthetic purity and realism; and between the Neoclassical and Modernist traditions in the fine arts". And, because I evidently represented the end of one era and the beginning of another, he suggested — no doubt thinking of a donation to his own museum — that I should be "given a permanent home at a public institution where I could be viewed by as many people as possible".

The opening of *Master of Marble, Antonia Canova's Greatest Sculptures* was a crush-and-gush affair. During the speeches the curators, the handlers and the installation team who had done the lion's share of the work shuffled their feet while they watched the chair of the board and director of the museum share the limelight. There was plenty of champagne — or at least prosecco, courtesy of the Italian Embassy. And there were enough canapés to provide dinner for those who hadn't been invited to the post-exhibition-opening feast.

True to John Clare's prediction, I was the center of attention. And in line with Kate's fears, I was also the center of speculation. Which member of the Simoni family did I actually represent? Who had brought me from Italy to Great Britain? How did I end up in a junk shop the present owner claimed to have bought me for a few pounds? And was it really true that every member of the Simoni family had perished at Auschwitz during the Second World War?

Kate Ames heard every one of these speculations and comments. She couldn't miss them because even after the guests tired of looking at me and displayed more interest in talking, drinking and hobnobbing, she had remained alongside the uniformed gentleman who was guarding my plexiglass box. No wonder she was relieved to have me back on her desk when the exhibition closed. But I didn't remain there for long.

***

There were many theories about who took me from Kate's desk a few weeks after I had returned from New York. Some said that a disgruntled Italian nationalist wanted to repatriate me to Italy. Others opined that it was no use trying to find me because, long before Kate had entered her office on the morning that she discovered I was missing, I'd surely have been on the midnight flight to Asia. Still others wondered if a member of the Simoni family had survived the horrors of the Holocaust and was furtively asserting their claim to ownership.

None of these speculations proved to be correct. Instead, when Kate travelled to Italy on her next holiday, I was in her carry-on luggage. Indeed, I was her only companion, as I had often been since she had broken off her relationship with John Clare. Once it became clear that the Canova would not be donated to his museum, Clare had not only lost interest in his fiancée, but was denied the half-promised promotion.

The port of Carrara wasn't the most attractive place to spend a week in Italy. Most tourists went to Marina di Pietrasanta or to Viareggio for sun and fun. But Kate wasn't looking for a beach-side holiday. She was on a mission to find salvation: by saving her recently deceased father's reputation, by avoiding the responsibility of owning an object she could neither afford to insure nor to maintain at museum standards. My owner also wanted to save me from becoming an object of worship. After all, Kate knew, as she took me out of her hold-all and caressed my back, I was only a stone, albeit a rather attractive piece of Carrara marble at that.

It was clearly time for Kate and me to part company, as I discovered when I was summarily thrown in a large arc above Kate's head and landed in the translucent water of the Marina di Carrara. Her gesture marked the end of our romance. As I sank to the bottom, I passed human waste, plastic bags, tin cans and bits of cardboard. Within a week my body would turn brown; and after that, just like the other pieces of long-discarded marble surrounding me, I would be covered from head to toe with a black crust that no amount of baking soda or scrubbing could remove.

For Kate, my demise was a liberation of sorts; for me it was a homecoming of sorts, a final metamorphosis. She had returned me to my natural marine habitat, where I had begun my life as a shell.

Private Enterprise

It seems remarkable to us today that a town of some 10,500 inhabitants lying in the heartland of the rural English-speaking Quebec, should have a purpose-built art gallery within the grounds of its local university. Writing this in 1961, I am all too conscious of the public scandal that has recently tainted us all; but I think I ought to tell the real story as I saw it at the time, step by step, incident by incident and reaction by reaction. This is because I am struck by the unique circumstances that brought it about, all within a period of under ten years. The unlikely series of events made a huge impression locally during an era when the world at large was more concerned with matters of life and death on both sides of the Iron Curtain that divided Europe.

To many people in the small town, I think it's fair to claim, it was the founding of the art gallery that opened a new window on to the world. They thought it was extraordinary that a former Canadian ambassador and his wife had not only funded the building itself: they had provided the resources to stock it with paintings, drawings, prints and sculptures acquired during their postings in Tokyo, Rome and London.

Of course, Harvey and Eleanor Smyth's wealth had not come from the salary of a civil servant, but had been generated by the extraordinary success of Smyth Investments. Often seen as a pioneer investment house in the financial markets of North America, the company had been Harvey Smyth's brainchild and its expanding assets became a legacy that outlived him. 'Private enterprise,' Harvey Smyth was known for saying, 'that's the whole secret, you know!' The philanthropy that he and Eleanor practised from the proceeds of their ever-expanding portfolio in the years following the Second World War set the seal of public approval upon this philosophy.

The Smyth Gallery and the town's university became the prime beneficiaries, despite Harvey Smyth's sudden death in 1951. It was later in the same year that its management was formalised with an advertisement for the gallery's first full-time director. And that's when I, Ronald Lee, had the audacity to apply for the job.

Prior to my own interview for this position, I was shown around the gallery. Among the vast collection were sorrowful Gothic wooden sculptures, illuminations of sacred Islamic texts, lodge books and psalters, all painted in tempera and adorned with thin sheets of gold leaf. Beyond the Middle Ages, I was stunned to find not only a fresco by Masaccio but also the wooden model of the dome that Michelangelo had designed for Saint Peter's Basilica in Rome.

Leapfrogging from the Renaissance to the seventeenth century, I marvelled at the realistically rendered paintings of domestic interiors that celebrated the newfound wealth of the Dutch Republic's bourgeoisie — wondering if the Smyths saw them as model predecessors.

Then there was the eighteenth-century collection of intricately painted seascapes of Venice by Canaletto and Guardi. And, by contrast, the nineteenth century offered light-filled landscape paintings by J.M.W. Turner, first edition wood-cut prints by Hiroshige and paintings by van Gogh and the French Impressionists. And that was not all. Although Harvey and Eleanor Smyth clearly favoured representational art, they had not shied away from collecting work by the twentieth century's early modernists. And they had even bought work from African artists, Aboriginal sand painters and Inuit sculptors.

During my interview for the directorship of the Smyth Gallery in 1951, the university president, who was chair of the appointments committee, asked me what I thought of the collection I had just viewed. I made it clear that I was enormously impressed. But I felt bound to say that, if the collection had been assembled by museum curators, it might have included a painting or two by Rembrandt, Rubens and their Baroque contemporaries. Looking at the other end of the art-historical spectrum, I wondered aloud why the astute collectors hadn't acquired work from Montreal's

Automatistes who were now giving New York's Abstract Expressionist painters a run for their money. Even so, as I told the university president at the conclusion of the interview, the Smyth Gallery was unique because Harvey and Eleanor Smyth had assembled an art collection mirroring their own tastes and their own predilections. It was, I boldly concluded with a flourish, an example of private enterprise in action.

****

As the third-generation son of Chinese immigrants who had worked on the railway in British Columbia then moved west to Saskatchewan where they ran the only restaurant in town, I was as much an anomaly in the small prairie town as I was later in the art gallery world. I had been out of place at the University of Toronto where I did my undergraduate degree and later at London University's Courtauld Institute where I topped that up with a master's degree in art history. And when I returned to Canada and became the curator of sixteenth and seventeenth century Baroque painting at the country's largest public art gallery, I had felt out place there, too.

The fact was I had applied for the directorship of the Smyth Gallery because my position in Ottawa had come to a dead end. I had little affinity with my predominantly French-speaking colleagues. My efforts to master their patois had met with limited success. Though I had made a few close friends, I had no family or romantic connections to keep me in the nation's capital. But the main problem had been my boss.

I didn't get on with the museum's director, Cyrus Cole, who had earned his credentials by moving up the bureaucratic ladder in Ottawa, not by studying at Europe's finest art schools. He disliked me. And even more, he disliked Baroque painting, of which I was chief curator. 'Lee's gallery is nothing more than a corridor linking the popular Renaissance to the Neoclassical galleries.' The crunch came when Cyrus Cole severely reduced my budget. That's when I felt that it was time to move on.

***

I must have shown sufficient enthusiasm over Harvey and Eleanor Smyth's collection and demonstrated how I could help the gallery become a first-class venue because the university president and his board offered me the job. When I got the news, I picked up stakes in Ottawa and moved to Quebec as fast as I could.

During my first month as director of the Smyth Gallery I was given wide discretion in assembling its board. Henry Brown, a well-known businessman who was looking for a bit of culture to raise his chances of becoming the town's next mayor, was an obvious choice, at least in his own eyes; and I went along with this. Harvey Smyth's widow, the petite Eleanor, was another obvious choice. And so, it seemed to me, was the man I myself put forward from the Department of Fine Art.

I had never encountered anyone like Tibor Nagy — not even in the hallowed halls of the Courtauld Institute in London — let alone in rural Saskatchewan or in oh-so-boring and politically-correct Ottawa. Tibor spoke no fewer than seven languages. He had published over twenty books on Baroque painting — albeit none of them in English. And that was not all that drew my attention to the art historian. Tibor was the best-dressed man on campus. While most of us wore navy blue blazers, grey trousers and striped ties every day of the year, Tibor dressed for the season. In summer he chose off-white linens. In the autumn Tibor donned rust-brown Harris Tweed jackets. In winter he wore a grey double-breasted, handmade Italian suit with contrasting tie and handkerchief. And just before the snow began to melt in April, Tibor announced the oncoming of spring by strutting across campus in a light wool, robin's egg blue suit. Variously attired, then, Tibor dominated the lecture halls, the faculty meetings and the dinner parties where he was treated by his hostesses like an exotic flower.

For those in the know, Tibor's manner of dress, along with his sharply pointed goatee, might have suggested an imitative younger version of the famous art historian, Bernard Berenson, for Tibor had not yet turned fifty. But nobody at the Smyth Gallery, with the exception of myself, seemed familiar with how the twentieth century's most famous connoisseur of Renaissance painting looked, and I was certainly not going to blow Tibor's cover. Because in Tibor Nagy I had found a fellow spirit for the first time in my career.

I can't recall the number of hours we spent examining his vast collection of black-and-white photographs of sixteenth and seventeenth paintings that he had taken in art galleries across Europe during the years before the Second World War. Crouched on a Persian carpet in my palatial office, we sorted the glossy photographs according to era, artist and school. I immediately saw that Tibor possessed an unerring eye. He wasn't afraid to use his intuition and draw on his memory and his experience in making an attribution. And I was duly impressed.

I not only learned a lot from Tibor Nagy. With no bureaucrats looking over my shoulder and no uncongenial colleagues, one might have said that Ronald Lee blossomed. I even broke my confirmed bachelor status by becoming more than friendly with the gallery's registrar, May Lum. Everything was going so well for me, personally and professionally alike, that I felt confident in proposing a new direction for the gallery's collection by exploring the work of the contemporary artists right under my nose.

I spent several weekends in Montreal visiting the studios of Marcel Ferron, Paul-Émile Borduas, Marcel

Barbeau and other members of Les Automatistes. I bought some of their work and put it on show in a special Christmas exhibition. Eleanor Smythe, who might have worried about how I was spending her money, raised no objections; Tibor tolerated my modernist whims; while the third member of our board, Henry Brown, strutted around the gallery on opening night as though he had found the key to the Holy Grail. During the ensuing weeks, Henry made his own collecting trips to Montreal. Abstract-Expressionist paintings suited his white-wall Bauhaus-style home. And his pocketbook, for they were dirt cheap in the 1950s.

By the end of the academic year, I had not only won the confidence of the gallery's board. I had developed a personal bond with every work in the gallery, making me reluctant to leave the premises at the end of the day. It wasn't the possibility of a break-in that kept me awake most nights, for we had just installed a foolproof security system. Or the excitement of having discovered Les Automatistes. My night-time thoughts imagined the people depicted by painters and sculptors come to life. I saw them dancing through the galleries, arguing with one another about where I'd hung them. I even heard them criticizing how they had been portrayed by the artists who had created their likeness. And, just before dawn, I watched them playing a joke on me by climbing back into the wrong painting. Yet, when I returned to the gallery the following morning, I invariably found that no sugar-plum fairy had brought them to life during the early hours of the morning since every work, and every figure in it, appeared to be in its proper place.

It was with pride and with hope that I wrote my first annual report. But there was one thing missing. I was no nearer to filling one notable gap in the collection: Baroque painting. It hadn't been without trying. I sought advice from my colleagues at America's leading institutions about how I might do so. They directed me to Christie's and Sotheby's auction houses in London and New York. But few paintings by Baroque artists came onto the auction block in the early 1950s and those that did were either beyond the gallery's acquisition budget or had been produced by minor artists.

***

Just as I was about to admit defeat, Tibor Nagy revealed that he was planning to make his first visit to Hungary since the outbreak of the Second World War. In the meantime, of course, his former country had undergone more than one drastic regime change, culminating in its effective subjugation to the Soviet Union, with a puppet Communist government installed. For Tibor, travelling to Hungary in 1953 promised both risk and opportunity.

His ostensible purpose was to add more images of Baroque paintings to his collection of black and white photographs. I suggested that he might not only take photographs but seek to acquire a Baroque painting for the Smyth Gallery. I had no difficulty persuading Henry Brown and Mrs Smyth to give Tibor five thousand dollars for the acquisition of a painting and a return ticket to Europe. Tibor's erudition, his former connections with galleries in Eastern Europe, along with his linguistic ability, gave him impressive credentials. And I saw him off at the end of the academic year with high hopes.

My belief that I was taking the gallery in the right direction was confirmed when I had a telephone call from Tibor at the end of the summer. He had just returned from Eastern Europe and had something to show me. It took me less than ten minutes to drive my second-hand Morris Minor from the gallery to a white clapboard cottage on the outskirts of town. When Tibor opened the door of the basement suite where he lived, his face cracked in irrepressible anticipation as the corners of his mouth rose towards his ears and his nose twitched. He led me into his sparsely furnished living room, then directed me towards a broad-bottomed chesterfield. Leaning against it were three large objects, each shrouded in material that resembled bed sheets.

As though pulling a rabbit or a bouquet of roses out of a top hat, Tibor removed one of the sheets with a flourish. I was dazzled. Before me was one of the finest examples of Baroque classicism that I had ever seen. Tibor didn't have to tell me who had painted it. The subtle gradation of colour and the soft light illuminating the low-life figures was the work of an Italian painter whom I revered: Michelangelo Merisi da Caravaggio, known by most people as, simply, Caravaggio.

Tibor presented the second work with equal panache. Painted by the period's greatest master of drama, movement and intense emotion, it was the work of the Flemish artist, Peter Paul Rubens. But Tibor saved the most accomplished work until the end of the viewing. The subject of the third painting showed an old man in deep contemplation. The modelling of the figure, the texture of the paint, the realistic rendering that captured the impoverished and destitute man, told me that this must be one of Rembrandt's last self-portraits.

After I had caught my breath, I took a closer look at the three works before me. All of them had minor imperfections caused by years of poor storage and, more recently, by being transported across Europe by train, then by ship from Hamburg to Montreal, with nothing more to protect them than a bed sheet. Convinced that the innate quality of each work transcended their shabby condition, I chose to ignore the tiny nick in the buttock of Rubens's voluptuous female, whose round coquettish face seemed to be looking directly at me in a cheeky "what do you expect" manner. I told myself that the battered frame surrounding Rembrandt's self-portrait could be re-gilded and that the slight bulge on the surface of the Caravaggio could be corrected by re-stretching the canvas.

The paintings could have been in worse condition. The canvases could have been scratched, discoloured or stained. They could have been retouched or over-painted. And the original varnish could have been removed from them in a clumsy way. However, during the course of the last three hundred years, every one of the paintings before me had survived substantially unimpaired.

Yet how, I wondered once I caught my breath, had Tibor managed to acquire works by three of the Baroque era's most celebrated artists. Even North America's foremost galleries had not purchased work of this quality. When I posed this question, Tibor shrugged then said: 'The Hungarians are so eager for hard currency that I got these for around fifteen hundred US dollars each.' Even in the early 1950s, these were relatively trivial sums.

***

It must have been at the beginning of my third year as director of the Smyth Gallery, that I decided to put our Rembrandt, our Rubens and our Caravaggio on display. In preparation for the exhibition the paintings were reconditioned and re-framed. And when we hung all three, they looked splendid — or at least Tibor and I thought so. Because when the show opened no one seemed interested in coming to see the gallery's newly acquired pictures. Rumor had it that attendance was low because some people objected to the gallery paying so much money for paintings that were second hand! But

219

not everyone was disappointed. After spending an hour with each work, the arts correspondent of the country's leading English-language newspaper, the *Globe and Mail*, was so impressed that she persuaded her editor to feature the paintings in the paper's weekend arts supplement.

After that happened, everyone took notice: the university's students, the local residents, the people from the surround townships, those living in Montreal and Toronto and even the editor of Quebec's conservative newspaper, *L'Action Catholique*. To accommodate the crowd, I opened the gallery during the evenings. I sent images of the paintings to art historians and journalists across the country. And I contemplated lending the paintings themselves to a museum in Toronto. And, this might have happened if the gallery had not discovered that the cost of insuring was well beyond their budget. Overnight, it seemed, the Smyth Art Gallery had become the envy of every curator and director in the country.

But it was my former employer in Ottawa who went one step further. Hailing the works as "national treasures", Cyrus Cole convinced his own board that our paintings should be on permanent display in the nation's capital under the care of a senior curator — the person appointed as my replacement. Only in this way, he claimed, could they be preserved to the highest museum standards and exposed to the largest number of people.

I responded at once by noting that the Smyth Gallery's lighting and temperature control, along with its security system, was first rate and that we had built storage racks in the basement using his gallery as a model. Undeterred, Cyrus Cole took his concerns to his local member of parliament. A discussion as to whether a backwater gallery had the right to own "such national treasures" ensued.

Had the issue formally gone to Parliament, I fear that the Smyth Gallery might very well have lost possession of the three paintings Tibor had bought. Compared with art museums in the United States, Canada's major galleries had few significant works because they were late to join the collecting game. Moreover, founded by thrifty Scots, it was unlikely that Canada's captains of industry would help the country's major galleries catch up with their neighbors to the south.

When my former boss announced moves to "appropriate" — the Rubens, Rembrandt and Caravaggio by moving them to Ottawa, my board dug in its heels. Reacting against Cyril Cole's arrogance, they made my own temporary position as director of the Smyth Gallery permanent. They placed a five-year moratorium on lending our newly acquired paintings to any other gallery. Mrs Smyth put the icing on the cake when she gave Tibor a further five thousand dollars to purchase more paintings for us on his next visit to Hungary. She also gave half as much money again for the purchase of wooden crates to protect any future purchases from damage during Tibor's travel back to Canada.

Accordingly, at the end of my fourth year at the Smyth Gallery, Tibor returned to the Eastern Townships from his travels with another painting by Caravaggio and three works by the French artist Georges de La Tour. When I put them on display at the beginning of the academic year in 1955, La Tour's ability to animate his figures with light from a single candle or an open window, was seen to full advantage. No one ignored the new acquisitions this time.

Delighted by the attention and not a little proud that one journalist dubbed us the most exciting "boutique" gallery in Canada, the board voted funds — this time ten thousand US dollars — for further acquisitions. Moreover, the university immediately agreed to give Tibor Nagy a six-month sabbatical providing he spent it — and the money — collecting work for us in Eastern Europe.

***

All of this was done with my full approval — but little did I realize how I would come to regret my decision. My first qualm came when, just before Tibor left for Europe on his third collecting trip in January of 1956, I learned that he had been commissioned by my old boss, Cyrus Cole, to help them expand their collection of

Baroque paintings. I winced at the thought of Tibor's time and knowledge being put at their disposal. But the members of my own board were more charitable. They were happy to have national acknowledgment of Tibor's expertise as a specialist in Baroque painting and to see his own financial prospects improve.

True, it could not have been pleasant for him to live in the basement of a wood-frame family home where every footstep, cough, radio programme and flush of the toilet was audible. Equally, teaching at an undergraduate university with no prospects of mentoring bright graduate students, could not have been intellectually rewarding for a person of Tibor's stature. In the end I agreed with my board that Tibor was worthy of more than admiration for his debonair and exotic demeanour. I reluctantly permitted him to moonlight and wished him well for his next trip.

The consultancy fee that came to Tibor — from what I now considered the Smyth Gallery's rival in Ottawa — indeed enabled him to buy a house of his own when he returned from his six-month sabbatical. Tibor's reputation also grew as did his prospects of gaining a position at a more prestigious university.

Indeed, watching Tibor move up the professional ladder in a discipline where preciousness and posturing so often triumphed over knowledge and hard work, stimulated my own ambitions. After all, I'd now spent over five years in the job at the Smyth Gallery where I had accordingly built up the collection and put the small gallery on the map. My own circumstances were much more comfortable, especially now that I was married to May Lum and settled in our pleasant stone-built home within walking distance of the gallery. But although I had been welcomed into this small community and given free-rein in my job, I secretly hoped that I would now be rewarded with a senior position at my former gallery in Ottawa or, preferably, at the Art Gallery of Ontario in Toronto — all providing, of course, that May was agreeable to the move.

However, my own chances of landing a position at a larger public gallery were eclipsed by external events when May and I watched the Russian tanks moving into Budapest on the screen of our black and white television. After Budapest's magnificent thermal baths had closed for the season in the early October of 1956, a student revolt was launched against the Communist policies imposed by the Soviet Union on the Hungarian government. By the time the Hungarian Uprising ended a month later, two thousand five hundred Hungarians were dead and another two hundred thousand had fled the country.

I could not have anticipated the impact of these events. For one thing, any hopes of acquiring more work for the Smyth Gallery were suddenly blighted because Tibor Nagy's chances of making further collecting trips to Eastern Europe seemed to be over.

Much more than my own career prospects were also at stake, as I had the grace to recognise. And when

I had learned that Canada was one of two countries that were accepting refugees, and that one Hungarian family had already moved to our small town, I had immediately contacted them. That is how I came to offer Janos Frank a janitorial position at the Smyth Gallery. Although this was well below his qualifications as a graduate of Budapest's prestigious Eötvös Loránd University, Janos was happy to have work to support himself and his young family.

The presence of one Hungarian at the Smyth Gallery had proved exotic. The presence of two, however, was to prove explosive. When I introduced the two expatriates, Tibor and Janos were like two dogs at a fire hydrant. They sniffed. They moved in a circle around one another. They stared each other in the face. Then they walked in opposite directions. I was concerned. Had I alienated the most valuable member of my board, not to mention my source of paintings, by employing Janos Frank?

When I raised this concern directly with Tibor, he gave me his now famous shrug, then reassured me that all was well. And when I asked if the Hungarian Revolution meant an end to his visits to Eastern Europe, Tibor likewise reassured me that the Hungarian Embassy in Ottawa had granted him a visa for his forthcoming trip at the end of the academic term. 'Art and politics have always been separate entities in my country.' Or so he led me to believe.

Tibor thus spent the entire summer of 1957 in Eastern Europe. This time, however, it was my former employer at the public gallery in Ottawa who offered to cover his expenses and to provide the crates for any purchases. And, not surprisingly, when Tibor returned at the beginning of the new academic year, he announced that he had just accepted a job at the University of Ottawa. I was about to lose a soulmate and a teacher, for there was no one else in the country who shared my love of Baroque painting. And there was something else: there appeared to be a conflict of interest. Before we could display the three equally distinguished works that Tibor had bought for us on his latest collecting trip to Hungary, news broke that Tibor Frank had acquired no fewer than eighteen paintings for our rival gallery.

I was furious. So were Mr Brown and Mrs Smyth who held me responsible for giving Tibor permission to collect paintings for the Ottawa gallery in the first place. In retrospect, it seemed an obvious mistake to allow him to acquire work for another gallery. Clearly my feeling of loyalty towards Tibor had not been reciprocated.

Tibor Frank's departure thus put an end to the Smyth Gallery's further acquisition of Baroque paintings. As the gallery's director, I found myself no longer the golden boy from the prairies; no longer an obvious candidate for promotion to a new position elsewhere. Resigned to the fact that I was now on a course as husband, soon-to-be father and debtor of a large mortgage, I agreed with May that we should be content with what we had.

***

It was not long after Tibor's departure that May invited Janos and his fair, small-boned wife Lena to our home for dinner. While Janos talked mainly about Hungarian politics, it was Lena Frank who had more to say about how much she admired the Baroque paintings that had been acquired by the Smyth Gallery. Yet it was only towards the end of the evening that Janos prompted Lena to reveal that before fleeing Hungary she had completed a doctoral dissertation on the French, Italian and Flemish artists who had flourished during the Baroque era. It was then that I asked her what she had heard of Tibor Nagy during the course of her studies.

I immediately regretted asking the question. Perhaps Hungarian scholars would consider him to be a fraud or a blow-hard? After all, he would not be the first person to fake his Ph.D. and concoct an elaborate list of publications. Maybe he had acquired the paintings in our collection by dubious means? Might Lena's discretion inhibit her from revealing too much — or would she tell May and me that the works Tibor had bought for the Smyth Gallery were not what they purported to be? And what would I do then: devote a special room to fake and misattributed works of art? Or would I sweep the matter of authenticity under the

227

carpet and hope that no other expert on Baroque painting would spill the beans?

My trepidation, I suppose, revealed my own suppressed doubts regarding my expertise as a scholar of Baroque art along with my failure to ask hard questions at an earlier point. Tibor had indeed provided the board with documentation showing that the Rubens and the Caravaggios had come from the holdings of museums in Budapest. Surprisingly, though, I had failed to press him hard enough on how or where he had found the other paintings that he had acquired for the Smyth Gallery.

But I had not, as I had feared, opened Pandora's box when I had asked Lena to tell me about Tibor. Even so, I was not wholly unprepared for what the young woman had to tell me. 'He bought most from the Hungarian National Museum,' she explained. 'They need money for, how do you say, repairs to the building, restoration and so on…' Relieved that the paintings we had purchased were, in Lena's view, authentic, I was nevertheless disturbed when she told me that every one of them had been acquired in 1919 during the short lived Hungarian Soviet Republic. It seemed that everyone in Hungary's art circles knew that Tibor had been the protégé of Friedrich Antal who had "liberated" our pictures along with other paintings from private collections at that time. 'This is how Hungary's National Gallery built its fine collection,' Lena added shamefully, 'and why I had such a rich source for my study.'

What Lena did not tell me was that, in selling such works to the Smyth Gallery, the present Hungarian government not only got hard currency in return, they also avoided retrospective claims from the rightful owners of paintings.

Everything I learned from Lena Frank as we sipped our coffee after dinner thus fell into place in my mind with an immediate sense of conviction, confirming suspicions that I had long suppressed. Knowing that without Tibor it was now unlikely that we would ever add another Baroque painting to our collection, I decided to celebrate what we had already.

***

Tibor Nagy had never found the time to write anything about the paintings he had acquired for the Smyth Gallery. So, I asked Lena if she would provide a provenance for every Baroque painting in our collection, then curate an exhibition featuring the work and oversee the publication of an exhibition catalogue.

'If I can do all myself?' she replied, her blonde eyebrows arched like down-turned parentheses. I took this as an acceptance on the implicit condition that the only other Hungarian expert on Baroque painting in Canada would have no say in the show. This didn't pose a foreseeable problem. Tibor was no longer on my board.

He was now living in Ottawa. And spending more time in Eastern Europe where he was continuing to collect paintings for our rival gallery than in the classroom at the University of Ottawa.

When I read about Tibor's acquisitions for our rival gallery, I gritted my teeth then put all of my energy into helping Lena make her exhibition a success. I employed an English tutor to improve her English. I arranged for a nanny to look after her two young children. And I sent her to my old stomping grounds. I wanted Lena to compare the paintings previously acquired by Tibor for the Smyth Gallery with those he had recently bought for the gallery in Ottawa. I even suggested that she might persuade them to lend a few of their recently acquired paintings to the exhibition she was mounting. Of course, I hoped that after viewing the paintings in Ottawa, Lena would tell me that ours were of a higher quality — and perhaps also discover that ours had been purchased for a lower sum. All of this was, I admit, a face-saving strategy on my part.

Lena did not tell me what she thought of the paintings she viewed in Ottawa. She simply said that they would not be part of her own exhibition. And that was that.

Our conversations during her frequent visits to the Smyth Gallery centred on how our own exhibition would be mounted. What should be the dimensions and length of the exhibition catalogue? How should we hang the paintings — in chronological order or group them by the artist? Should they be confined to the main gallery, or given more space by letting them spill into the wings? And if the exhibition was a success, should we extend our opening hours and hire an extra gallery attendant?

Since we had not replaced Tibor on the Smyth Gallery board, its membership was now down to two. I had their full support for Lena's exhibition. Henry Brown showed heaps of enthusiasm, which was good for my morale. More tangibly, Mrs Smyth readily came up with funds to ensure that every work that appeared in the exhibition would be illustrated in the catalogue and that before any painting was hung on the wall it would be given an elaborate gold leaf frame.

Lena's exhibition, simply called *Baroque Art at the Smyth Gallery,* did the paintings proud. It reflected credit on the gallery and the city too. On the opening night, the town's new mayor, Henry Brown, introduced a stage-shy Lena to the four or five hundred souls who had come to help us celebrate the occasion. Reluctantly, she mounted the podium, took a deep breath, grasped the hand-held microphone and, after giving it a few taps, announced that the pictures in our collection were, 'the best Baroque paintings in Canada.' May Lum and I raised our eyebrows. Had Lena meant to say "the best collection of Baroque paintings in Quebec" instead of in Canada? For, of course, our rival gallery in Ottawa, the country's capital, was not in the province of Quebec but in Ontario. It was, at least, an interesting slip of the tongue.

Or perhaps not. Suddenly I wondered whether this meticulous scholar was deliberately claiming that our paintings were of a higher standard than what Tibor had managed to buy for his new patron. After all, in acquiring our pictures, we had been given first dabs. Perhaps, on his more recent trips, Tibor had had to scrape the barrel. Maybe, I now wondered, if he had been forced to visit less prestigious galleries in his quest for further Baroque paintings.

Such speculations raced around my head overnight. But on the following day it quickly became apparent that Lena didn't need to justify what she had claimed in her short speech. The bad news for us was that every newspaper in the country chose to ignore the opening night of our exhibition; but this was because there was a much bigger art story dominating the newspapers.

***

While I had been officiating at the opening the previous evening, Tibor Nagy had been arrested by the Royal Canadian Mounted Police and thrown into jail. Maybe the charges against him did not rock Canadian society in the way that, in 1945, the defection of the cipher clerk named Igor Gouzenko at the Russian Embassy in Ottawa did, leading to the arrests of ten Soviet agents and kicking off the Cold War. Yet within the confines of the art world, at least, Tibor was viewed as the new Igor Gouzenko, albeit not a spy in the usual sense of the word. After all, there was no evidence that he had passed any secrets to a foreign country. But, Tibor had, as was now exposed, betrayed one of the country's foremost institutions devoted to art.

Over the previous two years Tibor Nagy had consistently falsely authenticated works of art that he acquired for our rival gallery. It appeared that all four works attributed to Rubens, in Tibor's confident authorisation, were not by the Flemish artist. Other paintings that Tibor had passed off as original masterpieces were, at best, "in the school of" — and in many cases blatant forgeries.

As head of the country's most prominent public gallery in the country and as Tibor Nagy's most enthusiastic supporter, Cyrus Cole was for once at a loss for words when the scandal broke around his head. He could no longer claim that his gallery possessed the best examples of Baroque art in North America and had acquired them without depending on the sort of private philanthropy offered by a Mellon, or a Hearst or a Morgan as was the case in the United States.

I watched as my former boss floundered from one misstep to the next in his humiliation before opting to take early retirement. Moreover, this was only the tip of the iceberg. Galleries in Western Europe and across North America successively discovered, when they took a closer look at the work in their collection, that they had been victims of similar scams, if not by Tibor Nagy then by other practitioners of these dark arts. The fact that hard currency was in every case exchanged for misattributed paintings thus made a big splash in Canada, the United States and across Western Europe.

Nearer home, I had another question. What had alerted Lena Frank to all of this? I listened to her story with an avid interest. It turned out that while viewing the works in Ottawa, she had immediately noted that, in what purported to be a work by the most celebrated artist of the Venetian school, Jacopo Tintoretto, the forger had used Prussian blue paint. Composed of ferric chloride, rather than derived from vegetables or minerals, this artificial pigment had been invented in the eighteenth century — two hundred years *after* Tintoretto's death.

Not every painting that Tibor had purchased for our rival gallery's collection of Baroque art was an outright forgery. Five paintings that Tibor had attributed to Rubens himself were, in Lena's view, by his assistant Deodat del Monte. Similarly, our rival gallery's Caravaggios were likely painted by the artist's boy-lover-painter, Cecco, who lacked the skill to obscure areas of the composition with dark shadows. And as for the two Georges de La Tours, they turned out to have been executed by Jacques Bellange, with whom La Tour had worked in the French town of Nancy. Every other painting that Tibor had purchased for the Ottawa gallery was the work of a contemporary forger.

Here was the explanation for the confident claim that Lena had rightly made in her talk on the opening night of our exhibition in 1959. Yes, as she insisted then, the Smyth Gallery did indeed possess the best examples of Baroque art in Canada.

And still does. Writing about all of this today, two years following Tibor's arrest, I remain the Smyth Gallery's director happily enough. I continue to enjoy Mrs Smyth's confidence — and the financial support of Smyth Investments. Moreover, with the assistance of Lena Frank as my chief curator, I'm continuing to expand the collection. I show visiting scholars interested in sixteenth and seventeenth century art our works which are stored in the bowels of our gallery. And when our Baroque paintings are on display, they are rightly viewed by those who, with Lena's magnificent catalogue in hand, come to appreciate an area of art history that they might otherwise have ignored.

As for Tibor Nagy, he still sits in an Ottawa jail, waiting for extradition to Hungary or possibly a spy trade to the Soviet bloc. I visited him last year, when I allowed our rival gallery in Ottawa to borrow one of our Baroque paintings. Surrounded by stacks of his black-and-white photographs, which he shuffled from one pile to the other, Tibor was dressed in prison overalls whose colour would not change with the seasons. Though I heard one guard refer to him as a dried-up little man and another call his well-trimmed goatee pretentious, to me

Tibor appeared content, declaring himself pleased that the pictures he had bought for us were being given the attention they deserved.

He said nothing about what had made him sacrifice his scholarship and his reputation by falsely authenticating pictures for our rival gallery. Was it a residual sentiment for the country of his birth? Or had he simply pocketed a handsome kickback? I like to think that it was blackmail or gentle coercion by the Hungarian state, rather than personal greed, that turned Tibor.

I have also asked myself why Tibor had never sold the Smyth Gallery either a fake or a misattributed work. And before I left the prison on that recent visit, I had my answer — or an answer of sorts. Because, within minutes of entering Tibor's cell, I was on my knees helping him classify his photographs. I had been co-opted into a shared task and a mutual enthusiasm for Baroque paintings — just as so often before. Perhaps he had not wanted to fool me. Perhaps he had not believed that he could have fooled me. Either way, I found it flattering.

Our rival gallery still makes noises about *their* "right" to own our "national treasures". But we know better. Perhaps Tibor Nagy's entrepreneurial instincts give a new dimension to the words of our benefactor, Harvey Smyth. 'Private enterprise — that's the whole secret, you know!'